The Secret Window

**Other APPLE® PAPERBACKS
you will enjoy:**

The Secret Window

Betty Ren Wright

AN
APPLE®
PAPERBACK

SCHOLASTIC INC.
New York Toronto London Auckland Sydney Tokyo

ISBN 0-590-33118-3

12 11 10 9 8 7 6 5 4 3 2   5 6 7 8 9/8

For George and my mother

Contents

The
Secret
Window

CHAPTER 1

The Dream Book

"Meg, for heaven's sake!"

The dream shattered under the impact of the angry voice, and Meg blinked awake. Her mother stood over her, filling the small bedroom. "What are you doing in *bed?* Are you *sick?* I *asked* you to peel potatoes and turn on the oven at four thirty. Is that such a big favor?"

"I'm not sick." Meg sat up and rubbed her eyes. "What time is it? I just lay down for a minute—I didn't mean to fall asleep." *The dream. Mustn't forget the dream before I have a chance to write it in the notebook.*

"Obviously it's five fifteen or I wouldn't be home," her mother snapped. "And I see no reason why a twelve-year-old girl needs a nap after school. When I was your age I was taking care of five little brothers and sisters while my mother worked. I certainly didn't have time to—" She stopped, her face going through one of the swift changes of expression that Meg knew well. "I realize you don't want to hear what I did when I was your age," she said in a softer voice. "Still, I can't see why you—"

"I'll peel the potatoes now," Meg said. "Right away quick. Should I make instant pudding for dessert?"

"That would be nice." Her mother followed her out of the bedroom, giving her a quick little pat on the fanny. "I'm tired, too," she said. "And hot. We all are." It was her way of apologizing.

In the kitchen, Meg carried the potatoes to the table next to the window so she could look out while she worked. Day's-end traffic filled the street. She could see a whole block of Brookfield Avenue from their fourth-floor apartment. Meg watched the Superette at the corner, where her brother, Bill, worked after school. She wanted to see him the minute he came out. She knew she'd be able to tell by the way he walked if he had great news to tell them . . . at last.

"Anything interesting happen today?" Her mother's voice was cheerful, the annoyance of a few minutes earlier firmly smoothed away. Her look-I'm-in-control-again voice, Bill called it. He said her sudden spurts of rage were little explosions designed to prevent the big one. "What big one?" Meg had asked, but he just shook his head as if she were too young to know.

"Nothing much," Meg said, her eyes on the street below. "I got a B-plus on the final history test. And Gracie stayed home with cramps. Her period," Meg added, just in case her mother didn't understand. It was irritating that her friend could spend a day a month at home with no questions asked, while her own mother made her go to school when she felt every bit as bad.

"And I'm going to be on the *Jefferson Flyer* staff next fall," Meg went on. That was actually very interesting news, but as usual her mother didn't realize it and changed the subject.

"I don't suppose Bill called," she said as she dipped the chops into egg and then into bread crumbs.

"No." It was Bill's news, of course, that her mother really wanted to hear. She had probably been thinking all day at work about the science award she hoped he'd win, and the university scholarship that went with it. She'd probably hoped good news would be waiting when she walked in the front door, news that would make her forget the unexpected heat and how tired she was.

"I'm pretty sure he's going to win," Meg said. "I really am."

"Little Miss Optimist."

At the other end of the block, the door of the Superette swung open, and Bill came out. He stood for a moment, then turned and started walking up the street toward the apartment building. Very slowly. A bad sign. If he had good news to tell he'd be running—well, no, Bill seldom ran, but he'd be walking faster and maybe looking up at the apartment windows to see if she was watching.

Meg's mother was peering over her shoulder.

"He didn't hear, Miss Optimist," she said. "Look how he's dragging. Or else he did hear, and he lost."

Meg longed to tell her mother about the dream she'd had just a few minutes ago, but she didn't dare. Even if her mother read everything that was written in the notebook hidden away in the bottom bureau drawer, she'd say the whole business was silly and only fools believed in dreams.

"I don't suppose you know where your father is."

Meg winced at the icy tone. "He's at the library," she said quickly. "He was here when I got home, but there were some things he had to look up."

"I'll bet," her mother said. "Funny how he's always at the library when his family comes home."

"That's not true," Meg protested, but she knew it was. Her father was a writer; he'd already had a book of poems published, and someday he was going to be famous. The trouble was, writing took lots of time, and lately her mother had become very impatient. And, though Meg tried to hide it, she was impatient, too. She loved and admired her father, and she wanted to be the daughter of a famous author, but sometimes she wished he'd stop writing for a while and get a regular job. For one thing, they needed more money than her mother was earning, and for another—

"You'd think he'd at least want to be here when Bill comes home," her mother said. "You'd think he'd be wondering if there was any news."

Yes, that was the second thing. They all needed to know he cared about them as much as he cared about writing. In the last year it had been hard to tell.

The chops were in the oven and the pudding was chilling in the refrigerator by the time Bill opened the door of the apartment. Meg met him and ducked as his hand reached to pull her single black braid.

"You didn't hear about the contest, did you?" she whispered. "Did you?"

Bill shook his head tiredly. "Nope. Not a single telegram, cable, or newspaper headline."

Meg gave a *whoosh* of relief. "We watched you from the window and you looked sort of sad. I think you're going to hear good news very soon, but—"

"But Ma was sure I'd lost," he finished. "Don't tell me." He went out to the kitchen and Meg followed. "Sorry, no big news today," he said. "How was the day on the real estate front?"

Meg's mother smiled at his teasing tone. It was the

first time she'd smiled since she'd come home.

"Well, no news is good news," she said, showing that she could be *Mrs.* Optimist when she wanted to be. "And my day on the real estate front was like any other day. Filing, typing, and looking for lost salesmen. I'd much rather stock shelves at the Superette and carry bags of groceries for nice old ladies."

Bill helped himself to a stalk of celery. "You wouldn't if you tried it," he said. "One of those nice old ladies swore at me this afternoon because I didn't move fast enough."

"That's terrible." Their mother dropped lettuce into the greens basket and turned the handle fiercely. "Did you run into Mr.—the principal, what's his name —today?"

"Corcoran, Ma. Mr. Corcoran. And, believe me, if he had anything important to tell me, he wouldn't mention it casually in the hall or the cafeteria."

"He'd call you into his office," Meg said. "And shake your hand."

Bill shrugged. "Probably. And he might call Dad and Ma to extend his congratulations for having such a terrific kid."

Their mother laughed. Meg, standing on one foot and then the other, felt left out. She doubted that her mother's face would ever light up for her the way it did when Bill walked into a room. Meg had to learn to accept the difference, the way she accepted having her father's straight hair and long feet. Bill and their mother looked alike—light blue eyes, curly brown hair—and they had fun together. No use asking for reasons.

When Bill left the kitchen, another celery stalk in his hand, Meg followed him down the hall to his bedroom. Maybe their mother had been fooled by his teasing, but not Meg. She knew he was unhappy, and she knew, the way she knew many other things about him, that he had just about given up hope that he'd win the scholarship.

"About the contest." She spoke in a whisper. He had thrown himself on his bed with his back to the door.

"What about it?"

"I have this funny feeling," Meg began cautiously. "I really think you're going to win the scholarship. I mean, I'm practically sure of it."

Bill rolled over and raised an eyebrow. "You're sure," he repeated. "Where did you get your information, smart kid?"

"I just know. I think maybe tomorrow is the day you'll find out. Mr. Corcoran will call you into his office and hand you a big tan envelope with your name on it in blue letters." Meg stopped, confused, as Bill stared at her. "I mean—I just mean that I have this feeling it will happen."

Meg waited for questions. She should never have

described the envelope. But Bill just yawned and fell back on the pillows. "Well, I hope you're right, old girl," he said. "Because if you're not, you're going to have me around for a long time. No prize, no college —and that's a fact."

"I know."

Meg slipped out of the room and closed the door behind her. Bill wanted the scholarship so much. He was smart and ambitious and he had to go to college. She understood all that. She even understood his wanting to get away from home'. And she wanted him to be happy. But she hated to think what it would be like when he was gone.

There'll be just me, she thought. *And Mama being crabby. And Dad waiting to be famous. And the dreams.*

Meg went into her bedroom and took the notebook from the bottom bureau drawer. There was a ballpoint pen clipped to the cover. She opened the book to a blank page and began to write.

June 8, 1982. Sunshiny hallway. Lockers on both sides. I look through an open door and see a man sitting behind a desk. He's talking to Bill. Gives him a big tan envelope and leans across the desk to shake hands. I yell, what is it? Bill turns around and holds up the envelope. His name in blue: William Korshak. He's smiling. I reach for the envelope and Mama wakes me up.

Meg started to close the book, then opened it and added one more line:

Mr. Corcoran has a mustache.

CHAPTER 2

A Big Explosion

Meg had been very little, maybe six or seven, when the dreams began. At first she'd taken them for granted.

Her mother might be surprised and annoyed at Grandma Korshak's unannounced visits from nearby Waukesha, but Meg usually knew when she was coming. She'd leave an extra hanger in her closet for Grandma's nightgown and clear a space on the bureau top for Grandma's hairbrush and false-teeth cup. Bill might be shocked when diggers and trucks rolled into the vacant lot down the block to destroy the only place in the neighborhood where he could collect insects and butterflies, but Meg knew they were coming. Her father might be thrilled because the Sunday *Milwaukee*

Journal unexpectedly printed one of his poems, but it was Meg who got up early that particular morning to fetch the newspaper from the foyer of their apartment building. No one seemed to notice that when others were startled, she wasn't.

When Meg was eight there was a fire early in January at the Pancinos' house in the next block. Meg, Bill, and their parents stood at the living-room window and watched the red fire-engine lights leaping and whirling through a curtain of snow. Tiny dark figures appeared and disappeared, and once a finger of flame glowed in the twilight. After a while her father and Bill went out to have a closer look at what was happening, and her mother went back to the blouse she was stitching on the sewing machine. Meg crouched at the window, terrified.

When her father and Bill returned, she ran to meet them. Their faces were red with cold, and there were snowflakes caught in her father's dark beard.

"Don't look so worried, Meggie," he said. "The Pancinos' Christmas tree caught fire, and the living room is a mess, but that's the worst of it. They think the cat pulled on the wires and caused a short."

"And guess what was the only thing Mrs. Pancino carried out of the house with her!" Bill's eyes sparkled behind his glasses.

Meg knew. "The cat," she said.

"Right!" Her brother pulled one of her pigtails. "You're a smart kid, you know that?"

He went off to his room, whistling, and Meg leaned against the couch, alone with her father. He was back at the window, shoulders hunched, hands thrust in his pockets.

"I knew about the cat and I knew about the fire," Meg whispered, almost hoping he wouldn't hear.

He turned to look at her. "Knew about it—how?" he asked lightly. His thin face was shadowed in the gloom. Behind him, snowflakes danced across the panes.

"I had a dream a couple of nights ago. The fire— and the snowstorm—and there was a lady running into the street with a cat in her arms." Suddenly Meg was sobbing against her father's jacket. "But I didn't see the house up close, and I wasn't sure it was Mrs. Pancino. It was just something that happened in a dream!"

Her father sat down and pulled her onto his lap. "Of course it was, baby," he said. "Dreaming about a fire is no big deal."

"But it was *this* fire," Meg sobbed. "I was standing in the snow and I saw the fire trucks coming."

"No, you didn't." His voice was still quiet, but it had changed. He sounded angry. Meg looked up and saw that his lips were tight under his beard. "Stop crying now, before Mama hears you. We all have times when we're sure we've seen a thing or done a thing before. It's just a trick the mind sometimes plays on us. Don't get so excited.''

"But I did dream it," Meg insisted. "Really and truly. And maybe if I'd looked hard I could have seen it was Mrs. Pancino and—"

"Now stop that!" Meg felt herself being pushed from her father's lap. "You're imagining things, and that's all there is to it. Listen to me, Meg." He pulled her around and lifted her chin so that she stared into his eyes. "Don't you say anything to Mama about this dream. She'd be very upset, and you don't want that." He let her go and stood up. "It's crazy to blame yourself for the Pancinos' fire just because you happened to dream about a fire, baby. *If* you did. So just forget about it.''

But, of course, she couldn't forget it. Her father had said *crazy,* and that was the word that stayed in her mind. It was crazy to have dreams that came true. If you talked about them it'd upset the people you loved and make them angry. She had learned something bad about herself, an ugly secret. That night she had been afraid to go to sleep.

About a year later Meg began the notebook. She'd had hundreds of dreams that year, but a few had been much more "real" than the others. And most of these "real" dreams had come true. Even though there wasn't another as terrifying as the fire dream, Meg became increasingly disturbed. She thought of telling Bill, but if he didn't believe her—if his voice and his face changed the way her father's had—she thought she'd die. She couldn't take a chance. And so, finally, she'd bought a spiral-bound notebook and had begun to write down the more vivid dreams as soon as she woke up. She'd chosen a book with flowers and birds on the cover, but that didn't make her feel cheerful when she wrote in it. Writing was just something she had to do because of her craziness. Three and a half years later, she'd filled more than half the pages. Many of the dreams she'd written down had come true; some had not. In a funny kind of way, the book had become her best friend as well as her greatest shame.

Meg's mind was on the notebook and the latest addition to it as she walked home from school with her friend Gracie Wriston the next afternoon. She could hardly wait to find out if Mr. Corcoran had called Bill to his office to tell him he had won the contest.

"You're not listening," Gracie accused her. "I don't have to let you in on this, you know."

Meg wrenched her thoughts away from her brother. "Yes, I am." She searched her mind for a clue to what Gracie had been saying. "Linda Bell's slumber party. You're the only one in the seventh grade who's invited."

"And I can bring one friend," Gracie said. "As long

as it's someone Linda likes. She's pretty particular, but I *think* she likes you."

Meg waited, not quite sure whether she was being invited or not.

"Well, do you want to go or don't you?" Gracie demanded. "If you don't, I'm going to ask Jean Monroe."

"Sure I want to go," Meg said. "But I have to check with my mother. If it's for overnight, she'll want to call Mrs. Bell and make sure it's okay."

"Of course it's okay!" Gracie's voice was squeaky with impatience. "If she calls Mrs. Bell, Linda will be furious. Look." She flipped open her math book and took out a slightly battered slip of paper. "Give your mother this, and it'll be all right."

Meg looked at the paper. It was a typewritten note saying Linda had permission to have a party and her parents would be home all evening. The note was signed *Mrs. J. Bell.*

"Well, I guess that's okay then." Meg slid the note into a pocket of her shoulder bag. "I'll tell her Mrs. Bell doesn't want to be bothered with a lot of people calling her up."

They had reached the front door of Meg's apartment building.

"I'm coming up with you," Gracie announced. "Your mother's home on Wednesdays, isn't she? You can ask her now."

Meg nodded reluctantly. "Wednesday afternoons. But she might be out shopping. I can call you tonight after I talk to her."

"I'd rather find out now," Gracie said. "If you can't go, I'm calling Jean as soon as I get home."

Meg gave up. Gracie was used to having her own way. But it could be awful asking about the party with someone else listening. If her mother was irritable or depressed, as she was most of the time lately, the answer was sure to be no. The chances for a yes were much better if Meg could choose the time carefully.

When they reached the fourth floor, Meg tried once more to change Gracie's mind about waiting for an answer. "I think my mother's gone out. I'm almost sure of it."

Gracie gave her a little shove toward the apartment door. "No, she's in there. I can hear her talking. Wow!"

Meg listened. It was her mother, all right. Meg couldn't make out the words, but the tone was too loud, too harsh for ordinary conversation.

"She must be talking on the phone," Meg said, and hoped it was right. But as she unlocked the door and pushed it open, her heart sank. This was no telephone conversation; the second voice had been too deep to be heard out in the hall. Her mother and father were having an argument.

"—sick and tired of it," her mother shouted. "I have

to do everything while you sit in here and scribble all day. It isn't right. I've had enough! It's time you make up your mind what really matters to you."

Meg panicked, turning to Gracie. Her friend made a little face. "It'll be over soon," Gracie whispered. "Don't worry about it. Let's go out in the kitchen and have a Coke."

Meg would have preferred to run from the apartment, but Gracie was already on her way to the kitchen. Meg followed on tiptoe with a quick glance down the hall toward her parents' bedroom. Her father was speaking now, his voice low, but angry too.

Then her mother started again. "I mean it! You can't have everything your way." Her tone was chilling. "Make up your mind what you really want."

Gracie went to the kitchen window and looked out while she waited for her Coke. "My mom and dad used to do that a lot," she said. "I was glad when he moved out."

Meg poured Coke into glasses, managing to spill quite a bit of it. Then she closed the kitchen door. "Oh, well," she said, trying to match Gracie's casual tone. "They'll be laughing in a few minutes." But even as she said it, she was sure it wasn't true.

"I'd go, except that I have to know about the party," Gracie said. "Do you think you could just run in for a minute and—"

"No!" If Gracie knew so much about family arguments, she ought to know this was no time to ask for something.

The bedroom door banged, and they both jumped. Meg winced as her mother's steps snapped sharply down the hall. The kitchen door flew open and crashed against the stove.

"What in the world!" Her mother's face was white, and her eyes were red and sore-looking. She took a step backward when she saw that Meg wasn't alone.

"Hi, Mrs. Korshak."

"Oh, hello, Gracie." She went over to the refrigerator and stood with her back to the girls, taking out covered dishes and salad makings. They watched until Meg couldn't bear the silence any longer.

"I'm invited to a slumber party at Linda Bell's Saturday night. Mrs. Bell sent a note." Meg reached for her shoulder bag and fished out the scrap of paper. Her mother crossed to the sink with a plastic bag of spinach, barely glancing at the note.

"I suppose it's all right," she said. Her voice was distant.

Gracie made an exultant circle with her thumb and forefinger, then scooped up her books. "I have to go," she said. "My mother'll be looking for me."

That was a lie—Gracie's mother worked the second shift as a hostess in a restaurant and was never home after school. But Meg didn't blame her for wanting to leave, now that the business of the party was settled. The kitchen fairly crackled with anger.

"Thanks for asking me." Meg followed Gracie to the door. But her anticipation of the party was spoiled. Of course she had wanted her mother to say she could go—but not that way. Not as if she didn't give a darn.

"See you tomorrow," Gracie said cheerfully. "We're going to have a terrific time, Meggie. Just wait!" She seemed to have already forgotten the argument they'd overheard. Meg watched her friend run past the elevator and down the stairs. She was in no hurry to go back into the apartment.

When she did, the silence was terrible, not at all the comfortable quiet she enjoyed when she was home alone. Her mother was still in the kitchen, and at the other end of the apartment the bedroom door remained closed. Meg stood in the hallway, yearning for a miracle. She wished desperately that they could all go back an hour. If only the argument had never happened!

She remembered what Bill had said about their mother's angry outbursts: "—little explosions that prevent the big one." Was this the big one he meant? Certainly something important, something frightening, had happened between their parents this afternoon.

Thoughts of her brother raised Meg's spirits. Maybe he'd know what was wrong and how to fix it. She went to the window and looked down the street. *Hurry up, Bill,* she thought. *I'm scared.*

Almost as if he'd heard her, Bill came out the door of the Superette. He looked straight up at the window where she was standing. And then he turned a cartwheel right there in front of the store.

It was such a surprise that for a moment Meg didn't understand what he was telling her. When she did, her heart seemed to stop.

"Mama! Dad!" She ran to the hall and shrieked in one direction and then the other. "Bill won! Bill won the contest!"

The bedroom door swung open and her father came out, looking tousled and unhappy.

"What do you mean, he won?" her mother demanded from the kitchen doorway. "How in the world could you know that?"

Meg was so excited that the words piled up in her throat.

"The window!" she gasped. "Look out the window!"

They followed her into the living room and looked up the street.

"Oh, dear God," her mother whispered, and it sounded like a tiny prayer. Because there was shy, unathletic Bill doing one cartwheel after another down the middle of the sidewalk, while passersby hurried to get out of his way.

If he *hadn't* won the science contest, he'd certainly gone right out of his mind.

CHAPTER 3

The Celebration

For a little while after Bill got home, Meg believed everything was going to be all right. Her brother hugged each of them, and they hugged him. He swung Meg around until she staggered. They all talked at once, filling the apartment with a happy sound.

We're a family, Meg thought. She looked at her smiling parents and could see no trace of the fury she'd heard in their voices just a few minutes before.

"We have to celebrate!" her mother exclaimed, giggly as a young girl. "Where do you want to go for dinner, Bill? The sky's the limit—within reason, of course." They all laughed.

Bill put a finger under his chin and rolled his eyes.

"The Firehouse," he said. "That's the only place that's wild enough and noisy enough to hold me tonight."

"Hurrah!" Meg hugged him again. Any other brother would have chosen steak or lobster for such a great occasion, but her brother wanted hamburgers at the funny old restaurant where they'd celebrated their birthdays for years.

Meg's parents shook their heads, but she was sure they were secretly pleased.

"Let's go right now," her mother said. "You can tell us all about it when we get to the restaurant, Bill."

A few minutes later they were out in the gentle June evening together, walking down the block to Corvell Avenue and then over to Main. Bill and their mother led the way, while Meg followed with her father.

"Well, this is quite a day!" he said. He sounded strained. Meg felt a tightness in her chest. Was he thinking only of Bill's wonderful news, or was he marveling that he could experience such happiness and misery all in one day? Now that the first excitement was past, his face wore its familiar private look once more. Meg watched anxiously as his eyes went from her mother to Bill and then to her mother again. What was he thinking? He wasn't really with them at all.

When they reached the Firehouse, her father seemed to relax again. They clustered inside the door to wait for a table. "What an asylum!" he muttered and ran his hands through his dark hair.

Meg and Bill grinned. He always said that while they waited for a table at the Firehouse.

"Oh, come on, Daddy," Meg said, because that was part of their tradition, too. "You know you love it here."

She loved the restaurant herself. The building was an old fire station, with a tower bell that pealed across the neighborhood whenever anyone pulled the rope. The waiters and busboys wore fire hats and plastic coveralls, and there were red lights that winked warnings from the walls. If it was a birthday, a waiter slid down the pole in the center of the dining room and delivered a free sundae to the birthday child.

As soon as they were settled at a table and had ordered, Meg's mother set her menu to one side and leaned toward Bill.

"Now," she said, "let's hear all about it. How did you find out you'd won? Did Mr. What's-his-name tell you?"

"Mr. Corcoran, Ma." Bill's thin face glowed as he recalled his day. "Mr. Corcoran called me out of calculus class this afternoon. When I got to his office, he acted more excited than I was. He kept clearing his throat and smoothing his mustache, until I wondered if I should leave and come back later. But then he said, 'Well, well, my boy, I'm not going to make a speech.' And he handed me this."

The envelope was tan. It was creased from being in Bill's pocket, but when he unfolded it, there was his name—William Korshak—in big blue letters. Bill held it up for each of them to see. Then he opened the envelope and read the letter aloud.

Afterward Meg could remember only the main points. The letter said Bill had won first place for his solar energy research project and for his high score on the National Science Clubs test. He was to receive a plaque at the state Science Club Sponsors' dinner and a full scholarship to the state university.

While Bill read, his voice trembling a little when he came to the part about the scholarship, Meg's mind raced. So Mr. Corcoran did have a mustache. And the envelope was tan with blue lettering just as it had been in her dream. She hoped Bill had forgotten her description of how the envelope would look, but there wasn't much chance of that. When he showed it to them, he had held it longer than necessary in front of Meg. Sooner or later he was going to ask questions.

"My son the scientist," their mother said, when the letter had been examined and put away. "I can hardly wait to tell everyone at the office." She turned abruptly to their father. "Aren't you proud of your son?"

"Of course I'm proud. Why wouldn't I be?" Both question and answer sounded harsh. It was the first time they had spoken directly to each other all that evening.

Bill looked at them with a puzzled expression. Usually he was the first to realize something was wrong, but happiness had made him giddy tonight.

"Here come our hamburgers," Meg said loudly. "Boy, am I hungry! I wish I'd ordered two of everything."

"And if you had, you wouldn't gain a pound," her mother said, going along with the change of subject. "It's terrible to have to sit and watch your skinny children eat tons of food. If I had French fries tonight, I'd be two pounds heavier tomorrow."

She made a face at her hamburger, which did look rather lonely without the French fries and onion rings the others had ordered. The tense moment passed, and they settled down to enjoy their food. But Meg knew that the party was not quite the same for Bill now. He had turned watchful, and there was a worried little crease between his eyes.

When they'd eaten their hamburgers and were ready for dessert, their father excused himself. Meg watched the tall figure cross the room, shoulders hunched, to talk to the hostess at the front desk. Minutes later, the fire siren shrieked, the tower bell rang, and their waiter hurtled down the pole in the center of the dining room. While the rest of the diners cheered, the waiter doffed his helmet in front of Bill and presented him with a towering sundae. A band of plastic-suited "firefighters" gathered around the table, and the entire room rocked as they sang "Congratulations to you . . ." off key.

Bill turned a deep red and clutched his forehead. The other diners laughed and applauded. It was a wonderful moment, and Meg was grateful to her father for making it happen.

One last time, she thought, and then she wondered, *One last time what?* The words had come from nowhere and refused to go away.

That evening Meg had one of the "real" dreams. Every detail was clear. But unlike most of the dreams in her notebook, this one had no familiar faces, and the setting was a place she hadn't seen before.

She was drifting down, down into a cave full of blue light. An odd sound throbbed around her, and she felt as if she were swimming through the sound and the light. Though the cave was full of people, she felt terribly alone. Figures came close, then drifted away. Meg looked around the cave, hoping to see a face she knew. Then her toe touched something—a bare foot with toenails that looked black in the blue light. A silver bracelet was looped around the ankle. Meg couldn't see the body to which the foot belonged or even—horrible!—whether there was one. She jumped backward and cried out. Danger —there was danger in the cave! She had to swim up out of the blue light. She had to get away.

When she awoke, her sheets were twisted into knots and her shorty pajamas were wet with perspiration.

Lightning lit the room, and the curtains belled out in the rising wind.

Meg untangled herself and went to the window to look out. It hadn't started raining yet, but it soon would. Down below, papers skittered along the alley and a cat cried like a baby. Meg leaned into the wind.

Danger, she thought. *Something dangerous is going to happen.* She was sure of it. But why a blue cave, why a bare foot? Until now most of the "real" dreams had involved situations she understood. The strangeness of this one made it more disturbing than the others. This dream was a warning. She hugged herself as thunder rolled across the sky.

"Meg, are you awake?"

She whirled around and saw that her bedroom door was open a crack. Bill's whisper was nearly lost in the roar of the storm.

"Hi." She reached over to turn on the bedside lamp.

Bill's hair was more tousled than usual, and his glasses were crooked. "I can't sleep," he said. "Come on out and make some cocoa."

"Okay." Meg lowered the window and hurried into a robe and slippers. What good timing Bill had! If ever she was glad to see him it was now.

But she almost changed her mind when she reached the kitchen and saw him slumped in a chair. The letter about his award lay on the table in front of him, and when she joined him he picked up the envelope and waved it at her.

"How did you know?" he asked bluntly. "Tell me that, for starters."

Meg brushed her hair away from her face. "I was just sure you were going to win, that's all," she said carefully. "You're so smart and everything."

Bill shook his head. "That's not what I mean, and you know it. How did you know what the envelope would look like?"

Meg took cocoa and sugar from the cupboard. "Most envelopes are tan—big ones, I mean."

"True. But what about the blue lettering? You said my name would be on the envelope in blue. Tan envelopes don't always have blue lettering, right?"

Meg knew that now was the time to tell Bill about the dreams. She could go to her bureau this minute and get her notebook full of dates and details. But the fear that he wouldn't believe her—or would tell her she was crazy—was very strong. Her father hadn't wanted to believe her, years ago. He'd become angry when she told him she'd dreamed about the Pancinos' fire. If Bill became annoyed or laughed at her, she couldn't bear it. Not now, when their parents were fighting with each other. Not when her dreams were turning into nightmares.

"I made it up." Her hands trembled as she stirred the cocoa.

She expected more questions, but he only nodded. "Well, that's what I thought," he said. "It's quite a coincidence, though."

"I know." She opened a box of graham crackers and put it in the middle of the table. She hated to lie to Bill, especially when she needed to share the truth with him. Now that he'd accepted her explanation, she almost wished they could go back and start the conversation again.

Bill pushed the envelope to one side. The chance to talk about the dreams was gone. "Then tell me this," he said. "What was going on at the Firehouse tonight? Dad and Ma acted—funny. You know what I mean?"

Meg nodded. Quickly she told him about the argument she'd overheard that afternoon. "It was awful! Not just an ordinary fight." She wished she could remember the exact words she'd heard. "They were really mad, especially Mama. She sounded so—"

"Fed up?" Bill's face was grim.

"Yes. Like everything bad was spilling out at once. I wish I hadn't heard it."

The cocoa hissed and boiled over the rim of the pan. Bill jumped up and lifted the pan off the burner. "Some cook," he said. "What would you do without me, kiddo?"

Tears blurred Meg's eyes. It was a good question. She dropped into a chair and stared at the formica table top, trying to imagine what life would be like when

Bill went away to the university.

Lonely. Scary. Sad.

When she glanced up, Bill was watching her. "I was just trying to be funny," he said. "It didn't work."

Meg shook her head vigorously, and he sighed. "I think we have a mess on our hands, kiddo," he said. "And I don't mean the one on the stove."

CHAPTER 4

"This Is Your Thief!"

"Meg, Gracie's on the phone. I can't imagine anything important enough to rate a call at six thirty in the morning—but what do *I* know? It's a long time since I was twelve."

Meg waited until her mother's bare feet slap-slapped back to her bedroom. Then she kicked off the sheet and hurried to the telephone in the kitchen.

"Is everything okay? Your mother sounded sort of strange."

"She was probably half asleep." Meg yawned into the phone. "What's wrong?"

Gracie sighed. "We didn't ever talk about what to

wear today. I tried and tried to call you last night, but you didn't answer."

Meg shook her head to clear away the cobwebs of sleep. Wear? What was she going to wear? Today?

Gracie sighed again, dramatically. "You've forgotten, haven't you? The field trip to the art museum, Meggie! With the eighth grade!"

"Oh," Meg said. "Oh, sure." How could she have forgotten that? They'd been talking about this trip for a month. And she was glad it was happening today. Gracie would be too excited to ask questions about the argument she'd overheard, and Meg wouldn't have to sit in class all day, thinking about her parents.

"Well?"

"My yellow top and the denim skirt," Meg said hurriedly.

"A skirt? You're wearing a skirt?"

"Didn't Mrs. Cobbell say it would be a good idea not to wear jeans, for once?"

"That's exactly the trouble," Gracie moaned. "I have this feeling the eighth graders will wear jeans anyway. I'm sure Linda Bell will."

For fifteen minutes the girls discussed what to wear. They finally agreed on yellow shirts and dark blue corduroys, just as Meg's mother appeared in the kitchen doorway.

A pretty good compromise, Meg thought, as she sat

down for breakfast a short time later. Mrs. Cobbell would be satisfied, and they'd have the fun of being dressed alike.

It was a subdued, uneasy meal. The only time Meg's parents looked cheerful was when Bill told them a photographer was coming to school to take his picture for the *Journal.*

Meg's father extended his coffee cup and toasted. "To our prizewinner and future scholar. We're very, very proud."

It was a solemn moment. Meg thought about it on the way to school. She wondered if her parents had talked in bed last night, and if yesterday's argument would begin again now that she and Bill had left the house.

Most of the buses had dropped their passengers by the time Meg reached the junior high grounds. Four remained, and Gracie stood in front of one of them, beckoning Meg to hurry.

"Come-on-slowpoke-Chris-is-saving-us-a-seat-in-the -back!" she shouted all in one breath. "We're leaving in five minutes. Look, I put my hair in a braid like yours."

The bus was warm and very noisy. Meg and Gracie moved slowly to the rear, stepping over the feet that darted out to trip them and ducking away from the jeers that greeted their look-alike outfits.

"Boys!" Gracie groaned, looking delighted. "Who

37

needs them!" She reached the seat being saved for them and dropped into it, next to the window. "I almost called you back to change it to the red shirts instead of the yellow ones," she said as Meg sat down. "Only my mother wouldn't let me call again. She was *so* crabby!"

"My red shirt is in the wash." Meg was grateful for Mrs. Wriston's crabbiness. A second phone call would have only made her mother more irritable.

Chris Svenson was a soft-spoken, pleasant girl who was always worried about her weight. As the bus started up, she turned around to admire the yellow and blue outfits.

"Neat," she said. "You two look like twins. My mother made me wear a skirt because we're going downtown."

"It's nice," Meg said. Chris was the only girl in the bus who was wearing a skirt, and Meg knew she was uncomfortable.

Mrs. Cobbell entered the bus, a bright-red wide-brimmed hat over her cotton-white bangs. She was a stocky person with a cheerful, often absentminded expression. Now she looked harried as she moved down the aisle, counting heads to see if everyone had arrived.

The bus started up and moved out into rush-hour traffic. As they made their way downtown, Meg thought about how dreadful it would be if Gracie or anyone else found out about her dreams. Wearing the wrong clothes would be nothing compared to *that* kind of differentness. She leaned back in her seat, glad that she'd confided in no one—not even Bill. Phrases from the last entry in her notebook flickered through her mind: cave . . . blue light . . . bare foot . . . danger. . . . *That's craziness,* she thought. *Maybe I really am—*

"Crazy," Gracie said, and Meg jumped. "Cobbell's crazy if she thinks we're going to walk with that bunch of—babies." Gracie looked at the seventh-grade boys, who had stopped teasing the girls and were trying to get the attention of passing motorists. "What a bunch of monkeys!"

Meg agreed. "But we'll have to walk with them," she said. "Mrs. Cobbell always wants us to stay close together."

"The eighth grade will be there, too," Gracie reminded her. "As soon as we start walking around the galleries, we can sort of edge in with them. I want to talk to Linda." She rolled her eyes. "Just two more nights until the slumber party. I can't wait!"

As it turned out, joining the eighth graders was not as simple as the girls had hoped. Mrs. Cobbell and the other teacher-chaperones seemed determined to keep the groups apart. As soon as the two classes had checked their jackets, bags, and cameras, they were separated and introduced to their guides.

"This is our docent, Mr. Peters." Mrs. Cobbell gestured toward the pale young man who stood beside her. "A docent is another name for a teacher. Mr. Peters will walk through the art museum with us and tell us about the artists and their work."

"Docent shmocent," Gracie muttered. Her eyes were on the eighth graders clustered at the other side of the lobby. "This isn't going to be any fun after all."

Meg hoped Gracie wasn't going to sulk. "I think our docent is handsomer than theirs," Meg whispered. "Actually, he's a pretty decent docent."

To her relief, Gracie began to giggle. Both girls covered their mouths and laughed until Mrs. Cobbell began talking about paying close attention to the lecture. Her soft blue gaze settled on Meg and Gracie as if she were speaking particularly to them.

The seventh graders crowded into the first gallery. The room was full of early American portraits, and even though the docent told interesting stories about the artists and their subjects, Meg thought the pictures were stiff and unappealing.

There was only one—a family portrait of a mother and her two children—that was interesting. The docent said it was likely that both of the children had died before the picture was painted. At a time when many infants died, mothers sometimes had their pictures painted with the family they would have had if their babies had survived. Meg's eyes filled with tears as she looked at the round sad faces of the mother and her ghostly children. Even Gracie stopped whispering to Jean Monroe and looked solemn.

"Spooky," Gracie said. Meg agreed. She was relieved when Mr. Peters led the class into the next gallery.

"I call this our dream room," he said. "The artists represented here depended on their dreams for many of their ideas."

Meg looked around and felt a rush of pleasure. The walls blazed with color in marvelous shapes. She felt as if she had stepped into another world, but a familiar one.

"Rousseau is over there," the docent pointed, and the class moved along a wall full of glorious animals in jungle settings too vivid to be real. "And over here is Chagall." Figures floated, arm in arm, over fairy-tale villages.

Some of the seventh graders giggled, and Gracie looked bored. But Meg pushed closer to Mr. Peters. She wanted to hear every word about these artists who actually enjoyed their dreams. Shyly, she raised her hand to ask a question.

"Were they really painting dreams, or did they just make up these pictures?"

The docent smiled. "Well, dreaming and making up things aren't that far apart. The artists in this room used their dreams for inspiration, and they used their conscious imagination to recreate them. Storytellers and painters dip into the same well as dreamers for their ideas, you know. Writing and painting and dreaming all help to tell us more about ourselves.''

Meg felt excited and confused. It was wonderful to think that dreams could be turned into paintings and stories—but what about "real" dreams, the kind that came true? Where did *they* come from? She would have liked to ask more questions, but she didn't dare. Some of the boys were already making faces at her.

"Dali is a dreamer, too,'' the docent said. The class looked at paintings of limp watches, floating bottles and fruits, and body parts. Meg thought about the bare foot in her last dream and the eerie blue light around it. If she had a choice, she'd spend the rest of the morning here in the dream room. She liked the way these artists accepted their own strange visions.

Mr. Peters waved them on into the next gallery, and most of the class seemed eager to move on. Meg followed slowly. She looked around for Gracie and couldn't find her.

"She sneaked back to walk with the eighth graders,'' Chris whispered. "Boy, is she something! If Mrs. Cobbell finds out, she'll kill her.''

Meg hoped not. But she wasn't altogether sorry Gracie had left; it was hard to enjoy the paintings when she knew her friend was bored. And they'd get back together when the two classes met for lunch.

For the next hour the seventh grade wandered

through one gallery after another. Remembering what the docent had said about the part dreams play in art, Meg enjoyed the paintings and sculpture more and more. She was admiring the shimmering color of a Monet garden when a burst of laughter came from the next gallery. Most of the class had already moved into the room. When Meg followed, she could hardly believe her eyes.

The room was full of sculpture. In one corner, on a two-foot-high pedestal, stood the figure of a Roman statesman. It was life-sized, and while it was clearly a man, dressed in a toga and carrying a scroll, the face was Mrs. Cobbell's. The wide eyes, the short, straight nose, the ridge of curly bangs across the forehead were all exactly like the seventh-grade teacher's. So was the bright-red wide-brimmed hat on the statue's head.

Mrs. Cobbell's face flamed with embarrassment and anger. Mr. Peters looked disgusted. Together they tried to quiet the laughing, cheering students, but it was no use. The laughter went on. Even though Meg felt sorry for the teacher, she had to admit that the red-hatted Roman was the funniest thing she'd seen in a long time.

A guard rushed in from another gallery, and the docent spoke to him in an angry whisper, probably wanting to know where he'd been while the hat was put in place. Then a chair was brought, and the docent climbed up and removed the hat. The statue became just a statue again. The docent handed the hat to Mrs. Cobbell and turned to the class.

"I don't know how this happened," he said. "But I hope whoever did it will never do anything like it again. This statue is very old. It could never be replaced if it were broken. The person who climbed up on the pedestal might have pushed it over and destroyed a real treasure. Taking a chance like that—and for a joke!—amounts to a criminal act."

A criminal act! The laughter died. The seventh graders looked at each other uneasily.

Mrs. Cobbell's color began to return to normal. "I don't see how anyone could have got hold of my hat," she said. "I checked it at the front desk when we came in, and I still have the tag the checker gave me. Here it is."

Meg felt a small flicker of worry without knowing why. Moments later, as they filed out of the gallery wing into a corridor leading to the lunchroom, a heavy hand came down on her shoulder. Worry changed to panic. It was the guard from the sculpture gallery, gripping her arm and talking over her head to Mrs. Cobbell.

"Here she is!" he said gruffly. He still looked sore and angry after being scolded by Mr. Peters.

Mrs. Cobbell stared at him. "Whatever do you mean?"

"I mean that this girl is the one who took your hat

and put it on the statue," he snapped. "I just talked with the checker at the front desk. She was away from the desk for only a minute or two, and when she came back she saw this girl coming out of the checkroom and running down the hall with the hat. This is the one. This is your thief!"

CHAPTER 5

Some Kind of Hero

"Did you do what he says, Meg?" Mrs. Cobbell sounded astonished.

Meg tried to pull away from the guard's grasp. "No, I didn't!" she exclaimed. "I wouldn't! I was right here every minute."

"Well, then the checker's made a mistake," Mrs. Cobbell told the guard. "Meg isn't the kind of person who—"

"Oh, that's the girl, all right." A woman in a blue smock bore down on them pointing a finger. "I saw her in the corridor. Long black braid, yellow shirt, blue pants—she's the one."

"I am *not!*" Meg squealed, trying again to pull away.

"I was right here with the class all the time."

"We'd better go to the director's office," the guard said. "All of us," he added, as Mrs. Cobbell and the checker began to argue. "What we have here is a theft from the checkroom and possible damage to a valuable statue. Those are serious offenses."

"There wasn't any damage done," Mrs. Cobbell protested. "The statue wasn't hurt."

"It could have been!"

Now Mr. Peters pushed through the crowd of excited students. "I'll take the rest of the class to the lunchroom, Mrs. Cobbell," he said soothingly. "If there's been a mistaken identification, I'm sure the director will get to the bottom of it."

He signaled to the class and led them down the corridor, while Meg watched in despair. *I wish I was a ghost like one of those children in the painting,* she thought. *I wish I could just fade away and turn into a dustball!*

The director didn't "get to the bottom of it" at all. He listened to the checker's accusation and to Meg's frantic denials, and to Mrs. Cobbell's assurances that Meg couldn't be the one. He asked Meg repeatedly if she had left the class at any time. He asked her if she understood the consequences had the statue been damaged. He asked her lots of questions, but he never once asked her if she knew of anyone else with a dark braid, a yellow shirt, and blue pants. And if he had asked that, Meg knew she wouldn't have told him.

When she finally escaped, after listening to a lecture on the importance of behaving like an adult in a building full of art treasures, she was furious. "I just hate that man and the guard and the checker, too!" she sobbed. "I wish I could go home right now!"

Mrs. Cobbell put an arm around Meg's shoulder and gave her a squeeze. "Let's just forget the whole affair," she said. "Don't let it spoil your day."

Spoil it! When they reached the lunchroom, Meg looked around. Half a dozen people waved and signaled her to come and sit with them, but she kept looking until she saw Gracie. Her friend—*ex-friend,* Meg thought—was at a table in a far corner with Linda Bell and some other eighth graders. All the girls were looking at Gracie and listening to her, as if she were some kind of hero. Then one of them noticed Meg, and they all turned to stare. Gracie waved to her and doubled over with laughter.

Meg stormed across the lunchroom. It was easy to imagine Gracie noticing the Mrs. Cobbell–face of the statue and deciding to steal the hat. Her eighth-grade friends probably thought she was terrific.

Gracie's giggles faded as Meg reached her table.

"Darn you, anyway!" Meg snapped. "You think it's really funny to get someone else into trouble."

Gracie tried to pull her down on the bench. "I didn't know they blamed you," she protested. "Honest,

49

Meggie! Chris told me just a few minutes ago. By then it was too late."

"Too late for what?" Meg demanded. "You could have come to the director's office and told him the truth. Some friend you are!"

Linda leaned across the table, her long auburn hair falling across her face. "Oh, forget it," she said. "Don't be a crybaby, Meg. Gracie didn't mean to get you into trouble. Be a good sport."

"I *am* a good sport," Meg said. "I just don't see why I should—"

She looked across the cafeteria and saw that Mrs. Cobbell and some of the seventh graders were staring. There was an odd expression on Mrs. Cobbell's face as she looked from Meg to Gracie and back again. She was noticing the twin look for the first time.

Now she knows, Meg thought. *At least, she's guessed. They all know.*

Meg felt her anger melting away. It was too bad to have the museum director and the guard and the checker believe she had done something she hadn't done, but her friends knew the truth. She felt much better, even a little heroic because she hadn't tattled.

"Get your lunch and come sit with us," Gracie ordered. "We're talking about the party. Wait'll you hear." She looked up at Meg with a grin. "I'm really sorry, Meggie."

And that was that. Gracie would never understand.

"It's okay," Meg said softly. Then she turned and walked back across the room. She wasn't angry anymore, but she didn't feel like sitting with Gracie, either. *I'm a good sport,* she thought, *but not that good.*

At the cafeteria counter Mrs. Cobbell joined her. "I believe I understand what happened now, Meg," she said. "If you like, we'll go back to the director's office and explain. Gracie, too."

But Meg shook her head. "It's okay," she said again. "I'd rather just forget the whole thing, Mrs. Cobbell."

Meg took her sandwiches, Coke, and fruit to Chris's table.

"We saved a place for you," Chris said. "See?" She pointed to a sign penciled on a napkin: *Reserved especially for Meg Korshak.*

Meg smiled wearily. "That's me," she said. She'd had more than enough of being somebody else.

CHAPTER 6

Terrible News

When Meg turned the corner and started up Brook-field Avenue, she saw a moving van in front of her apartment building. The looming shape swept away thoughts about the events at the art museum. Then she saw an unfamiliar green studio couch being carried down the ramp, and she sighed with relief. The van had nothing to do with her family. Someone must be moving into the front apartment on the second floor.

Meg walked faster, hoping to see the new neighbors, but there was no one in sight except the movers and a small skinny boy who stood nearby and watched with a bored expression.

Maybe the new tenants would have a baby and need

a sitter. Summer vacation was just a few days away, and Meg hoped to find a job. Most of the people she knew asked senior high school girls to sit for them, but a new family might not care so much about age.

Meg found Bill and her father in the kitchen frying sausages and making a salad.

"Ma has to work late," Bill explained. "She called and said we should eat without her." He looked uncomfortable, and Meg wondered what they had been talking about before she arrived.

A moment later she knew.

"This gives the three of us a chance to discuss a few things," her father said. "Things your mother and I have already talked over."

His face looked thinner than usual, and very tired. *I don't want to hear!* Meg cried silently, but she knew it would be useless to say the words out loud.

"This is hard to explain." Her father's deep voice filled the space around her. "But I want you both to understand. The important fact is, my work is getting better right along. I'm sure of it! The comments I get from editors are very encouraging." His voice trembled as he hurried on. "I think I have a very good chance of having a book published before long."

Was this what he wanted to talk about? Poetry?

"You already have a book," Meg said.

"Which I paid to have printed myself." Her father shook his head, as if the book had been a foolish mistake. "Five years ago it seemed like a good idea—a way of reaching my audience—but now I can see it was a waste of money. I need the support of a major publisher to get attention."

He paused, and Meg knew he was thinking of the unopened cartons of books that were stored in the basement locker. Once in a while her father gave away a copy, but no one ever offered to pay for it. That was when all the arguing between her parents began—when those boxes were moved into the locker. It was right about then that her father quit his job to write all the time.

"Anyway, the point is, kids, your mother wants me to give up writing and get a job. I don't blame her," he went on hurriedly. "I don't blame her at all. She's been the money-maker in the family for a long time, and it's natural that she should get impatient. She'd like me to give up the whole idea. And the trouble with that is"—Bill dropped the frying-pan lid, and Meg jumped—"I can't do it. Writing is my life. It took me a long time to learn that, and now I have to live with it. Any way I can."

Writing is my life! Meg couldn't believe he had said those words. "What about us?" she whispered. "What about Bill and me? What about Mama? Aren't we your life, too?"

He put out his arms to her, but she stepped back, waiting for his answer.

"Of course you are. You mustn't ever doubt that. But I can't be a good father or a husband if I can't write, too. At least, I need more time to find out how successful I'm going to be."

Meg felt sick. How neatly he had it all figured out! How willing he was to let them go!

"So what's going to happen?" she asked flatly.

"He's going away." Bill was at the stove with his back to them.

"I called your Uncle Henry in Marquette this morning. He's going to let me live in the family cottage out at Lake Superior. And he thinks I can get some part-time work around there, helping out the other property owners. It'll be enough for food, and I'll still be able to write most of every day."

He stopped, waiting for them to say something, but Meg had no words for what she was feeling. *Writing is my life.* That was what he'd told them. Writing was the only thing that mattered. He could sit up there at Uncle Henry's cottage and write his precious poems and stories and feel like a whole person, with the bits and pieces of his family scattered behind him.

"I wish I could make you see this as I do," he said. "You feel as if I'm walking out on you, but there's more to it than you know. I wouldn't go if your mother didn't have a good job. Even Bill's scholarship—it's a kind of sign that it's okay for me to try this now." He looked pleadingly at his son's rigid back. "You'll get along fine. You're great kids. I want to make you proud of me someday, the way I'm proud of you."

"Let's eat," Bill said. He turned to reach for the bag of rolls on the counter, his face pale. Meg remembered how he'd looked at the Firehouse the night before. He'd been the happiest person in the world, and they'd been happy with him. Now the joy was gone, and there was nothing left but this, a family falling apart.

It was more than Meg could bear. "I'm not hungry," she cried and ran out of the kitchen, out of the apartment. She didn't care where she went, as long as she couldn't hear her father.

The moving van was gone from the front of the building, and Brookfield Avenue had settled into its usual dinner-hour calm. It was an old street, a mixture of medium-sized apartment buildings, turn-of-the-century houses, and small businesses. Meg sank down on the top step and looked around. She felt like a different person from the girl who had come home less than half an hour ago. Even the neighborhood—ordinary old Brookfield Avenue—looked strange to her. She wondered if anything would ever be the same again.

"Want a Coke?"

The husky voice came from overhead. Meg looked

up. The skinny boy she'd seen earlier was leaning from a second-floor window and looking down at her with a hopeful expression.

Meg wanted to say no, but there was something in the boy's manner that stopped her. "No" was what he expected to hear.

"I don't mind," she said stiffly.

A smile spread across the thin, freckled face. "I'll be down in a minute. Don't go away."

If I only could, Meg thought. She waited, staring into the twilight, until the door opened and a bottle of Coke appeared over her shoulder. She turned to say thanks—and stared in surprise. Was this the "boy" she had just seen? Lipstick. Pierced ears. A pale pink T-shirt with dark blue letters across the front:

GOD ANSWERS PRAYERS. TALK TO HER.

"Oh, I thought you were a—" Meg decided not to say what she'd thought. "I'm Meg Korshak."

"Rhoda Deel." The newcomer sat on the step next to Meg and stretched out her blue-jeaned legs. "I know what you were thinking. Everyone teases me about looking like a boy. It's because I'm so flat. The superintendent of the building said, 'Hi, sonny,' when we moved in." She looked down at herself and sighed. "My dad gave me this T-shirt for my twelfth birthday —he said I should be proud to be a woman. Maybe I will be someday. But right now I don't care what people think. If I did, I'd let my hair grow long and wear skirts—ugh! I mean, if you're going to worry about stuff like that, you're not going to have fun at all. Right?"

Meg listened and sipped her Coke. The lipstick and earrings suggested that Rhoda Deel did want the world to know she was a girl—at least, she wanted Meg to know.

"I wasn't sure I should talk to you," Rhoda went on. "You looked as if you had something important on your mind."

Meg didn't reply for a moment. Then, "I live on the fourth floor," she offered. "I guess that was you moving in this afternoon."

"Right. My dad was transferred again. We drove all the way from New York and got here an hour before the moving van. That makes four moves in three years. We're getting pretty good at timing the trips and packing and unpacking."

Meg was impressed. She couldn't remember having lived anywhere except on Brookfield Avenue in Milwaukee. *Lucky Rhoda Deel,* she thought. *Lucky girl whose father loves his family enough to take them along when he moves.*

"What's New York like? Did you see lots of famous people while you lived there?"

"Liza Minnelli once, on Third Avenue. And Carly Simon in a delicatessen. At least, I think it was Carly Simon." Rhoda frowned, trying to remember. "I guess that's all. . . . Oh, Dr. Christiaan Barnard, the doctor who did the first heart transplants. He gave a talk at the All-City Science Fair last year. I didn't win a prize or anything, but my dad and I went to see the demonstrations."

"My dad" again! This girl talked about her father more than anyone Meg had ever met.

"My brother Bill *did* win a prize in the national science contest," Meg said, feeling mean. "He has a scholarship."

"Wow!" Rhoda sat up and stared at her in open-mouthed excitement. "What kind of experiment did he do?"

"Something about energy." Meg already regretted her bragging. "Solar energy. I'll introduce you and he can tell you himself."

"Great!" Rhoda leaned back and tipped her Coke bottle, bottoms up. "I wish I had a brother. Or a sister. Or a dog. Just someone who'd be around, you know? It gets kind of lonesome with all this moving. Every new street looks pretty much like all the others to me —I just wake up one morning and realize all my friends are somewhere else."

"Maybe your folks didn't want any more children," Meg said. She was thinking of something she'd heard her mother say to a friend long ago. *Of course it's very nice to have a boy and a girl, but the second child in our family was strictly an accident.*

Rhoda nodded. "I don't think they wanted even one. Not my mother, anyway. She moved to Los Angeles a long time ago. She had to."

"Why?"

"To find herself." Rhoda said the words as if they explained everything. "She's an assistant to a very important film director. I'm going out to stay with her for a couple of weeks before school starts next fall."

Meg was stunned. How could Rhoda speak so calmly about her mother's leaving? She pictured her father upstairs, maybe packing his clothes this very minute, and her throat ached with the effort to hold back her tears.

She stood up. "I have to go. Thanks for the Coke."

Rhoda looked surprised. "What'd I say?" she demanded. "Did you think I was bragging about my mother's job? I don't care about *that*. We can talk about something else."

Meg felt the tears begin to spill over. "I just have some work to do now—homework."

"Oh." Rhoda continued to look at her. "Well, I'll see you later then, huh?"

Meg hurried inside and ran all the way up to her apartment without stopping. Maybe it was too late for Rhoda and her mother; Rhoda didn't seem to care much, anyway. But Meg's father was still at home. She would talk to him—make him change his mind. If they all worked together, maybe they could help him to find himself right here at home.

But when Meg let herself into the apartment, her father's bedroom door was closed and his typewriter chattered. She started down the hall, then hesitated. Bill's door was closed, too. She looked from one door to the other. If her brother didn't know what to do, what could *she* possibly say to change their father's mind?

She wandered into the living room and looked down at the street. Rhoda Deel was still there on the steps. As Meg watched, she leaned back, her Coke bottle clutched in one hand, and stuck out her tongue at Brookfield Avenue.

CHAPTER 7

The Brown Suitcase

The hall was familiar in every detail. The umbrella stand was there, the gate-leg table, the mirror with birds carved in the frame. Above the mirror a small diamond of pink light was reflected from the bowl on the table. The Tinker Bell light —that was what Meg had called it after seeing the stage version of **Peter Pan.** *She stared at the light, knowing that when she turned she'd see something else—something that didn't belong in the apartment hallway. Something she didn't want to see.*

There were voices in the kitchen and street sounds from the open living-room windows. A truck started up with coughing sounds. Meg pulled her eyes away from the pink light on the wall and looked down at the flowered carpet. The roses. The old ink spot that would never come out. Then, very slowly, she turned. A brown suitcase leaned against the wall, just inside the door.

A suitcase. Her father's? Meg was wide awake and out of bed in the same moment. She ran into the hall. There was no suitcase. Sunlight streamed through the open door of her parents' bedroom.

"Dad?" She went in. The room was unexpectedly neat for so early in the morning. The bed was made, and the top of her father's desk was bare except for the pencil holder she'd made for him in third grade. Her mother sat in the armchair in the corner. She was dressed and ready for work, but she just sat there.

"He's gone," her mother said. "He got up at four and packed and left. He didn't want any more good-bys—said he'd write when he got settled. There's a bus to Marquette at six ten." They both looked at the clock on the bedside table. It was five minutes after six.

Down at the bus station, people must be standing in line. Mothers and babies going to see grandparents. Old people going to visit their children. Salesmen with briefcases. Fathers running away from their families.

"I hate him!" Meg cried. "I really hate him!"

Her mother stood up and came around the bed. She hugged Meg. "I should probably tell you not to say that," she murmured. "But I hate him, too, at the moment." Her voice broke, and she stepped back.

"Let's have breakfast, kiddo," she said. "You wake up Bill. Life goes on."

Meg went out into the hall, where the image of the brown suitcase jumped into her mind again. Maybe her father had put it down outside her door, for a second, just before he left. Maybe he'd looked in at her. She was glad she'd been asleep. She didn't want any more good-bys either. She tapped on Bill's door, then went into the bathroom to splash cold water on her face and brush her teeth.

When Meg and Bill came downstairs after breakfast, Rhoda Deel was sitting on the front step. She was wearing dark brown pants and a plaid blouse, and her hair had been washed and brushed. She blushed when Meg introduced her to Bill. Most of Meg's friends didn't pay much attention to Bill; he wasn't a high-school jock, and they weren't interested in science. But Rhoda acted as if she were meeting a movie star. When she found her voice, she asked one question after another about the demonstration Bill had entered in the science contest. Soon they were talking like old friends.

Meg stood on one foot and then the other, wondering how Bill could act as if nothing were wrong. When he finally said good-by, the girls had to hurry to avoid being late for school.

"Boy, are you lucky!" Rhoda said. "Your brother's a really neat person."

Meg nodded. Her mind was miles away on a bus racing north to Marquette. She felt Rhoda looking at her.

"You feel okay, Meg? You seem kind of—quiet. Are you mad about something?"

"I'm all right," Meg said. But then, quite unexpectedly, she found herself telling Rhoda the whole story —about her father, about his leaving, everything. It all spilled out in a furious rush. "And I hate him!" she finished. "This is the worst thing that's ever happened."

Rhoda sighed. "He's finding himself," she said. "Boy, oh, boy, I know just how you feel."

Meg looked at her new friend gratefully. She'd been wrong about Rhoda. Rhoda remembered exactly what it was like to have a parent walk out on you.

"Want to know something funny?" Rhoda said. "I guess I saw him. Your father. This morning. I couldn't sleep—I always have a hard time sleeping the first few nights in a new place. So I got up and poured a glass of milk, and I sat at the window for a while. And pretty soon this man came out of the apartment carrying a suitcase and a briefcase and a typewriter. He had a beard, and he was wearing a blue jacket."

She waited for Meg's nod. "I'll tell you something," she went on. "I didn't know who he was, natch, but I felt sorry for him. He had a sad look. He kept glancing back over his shoulder at the building as he walked to the corner. Once he stopped and put down the suitcase and just stared. I thought maybe he'd seen me at the window, so I ducked down. And when I looked again, he was gone."

Meg blinked. She didn't want to see her father the way Rhoda had described him. "So that's that," she said. "Who cares, anyway! We'd better hurry." She grabbed Rhoda's wrist. "I'll show you where the principal's office is before I go to my homeroom. Maybe you'll be assigned to the same room."

"Actually I probably won't get a room assignment till September," Rhoda said. "They never want you to start classes so near the end of the semester. I'll just register today and find out where I am compared to the rest of the kids. And see if there's anything interesting to take in summer school."

They crossed the street to the schoolyard, and Meg began to look for Gracie. When she thought about what had happened at home, the trouble at the art museum no longer seemed important. She'd forgive Gracie, because most of the time Gracie was fun.

Meg left Rhoda at the principal's door with a promise to watch for her between classes. Then the first bell rang, and the school day started.

If Gracie was worried about being forgiven, it didn't show.

"Wait'll you hear," she squealed when Meg joined

her on the way to the cafeteria at noon. "Linda told me all about the party. She's having boys!"

Meg stared. "At a slumber party? You're making that up!"

"Of course not at the slumber party, silly." Gracie giggled. "She's having a boy-girl party first, and then some of us—her best friends—will stay for the slumber party. Wait'll you see her house!"

"What's it like?" Meg was trying to ignore the steady chorus of "who-cares" pounding through her brain.

It turned out that Gracie hadn't been inside the Bells' house, though she'd strolled past it dozens of times. She was going inside after school today, however, because Linda had given her a long list of errands to take care of before the party.

"I won't be able to walk home with you," Gracie said. "I'll be busy. I'll call you tomorrow."

Rhoda didn't come to the cafeteria. "There's a new girl in our apartment building," Meg said, but she let the subject drop when Gracie didn't comment. Rhoda and Gracie would never be friends anyway. Gracie would faint dead away at the thought of taking summer school classes for the fun of it.

The day dragged on. Meg felt strange—a person who hated her father and whose father didn't care. Yet no one noticed how different she was. Only Mrs. Cobbell looked puzzled when Meg replied "I don't know" to a perfectly simple question.

"I hope you're not still thinking about that business at the art museum, Meg," Mrs. Cobbell said, when class was over. "Put it out of your mind. *I* know you weren't involved in any way."

Meg thanked her and hurried away. Mrs. Cobbell was nice, but Meg didn't feel like talking to her. How could you tell a teacher that borrowing a hat and putting it on a statue was kid stuff?

The second-floor apartment window was empty when Meg reached home, but there were curtains blowing in the breeze, and spiky green leaves stuck up above the sill. Rhoda had been busy. Meg forced herself up the front steps and up the three flights to her floor. She stopped at every landing to stare out the window. What had Rhoda done the day her mother left for California? Had she wanted to run away—anywhere except home?

When Meg opened the apartment door, the first thing she saw was the brown suitcase. It stood in the hallway, next to the door, as she had seen it in her dream. For one second she couldn't move; then a coffee cup clinked in the kitchen, and she raced joyfully toward the sound.

"Dad!"

She skidded to a stop in the doorway. Grandma Korshak was sitting at the kitchen table, opposite Meg's mother, drinking coffee. A plate of cookies was set between them.

The suitcase wasn't her father's. Why hadn't she known that? He was in Marquette by now—probably telling Uncle Henry how glad he was to be there.

Grandma Korshak didn't notice Meg's disappointment. The tiny, dark old lady held out her arms for a kiss.

"What a big girl you are!" Grandma said. "Every time I come, you've changed. You're almost a woman now."

"She's twelve," Meg's mother said in a cold voice. "She's still a child. She's a child who needs her father."

Meg drew back. She'd walked in on something *again*.

Grandma Korshak shook her head. "You're scaring her," she said gently. "You mustn't worry her."

"*I* mustn't worry her! I'm not the one who's walked out. I'm not the one who's ready to give up everything for a selfish whim!" Meg's mother stood up, her face tight with anger and hurt. "You raised him, Mother Korshak. You encouraged him to believe he had talent, and now we have to pay for it. A happy, ordinary life isn't enough for him. Don't tell *me* I mustn't worry Meg. This family has plenty to worry about. She might as well do her share."

Meg's mother ran out of the kitchen and down the hall. The bedroom door slammed.

Grandma lifted her coffee cup in both hands and drank. Then she motioned Meg to the empty chair opposite her.

"It'll be all right, Meggie," she said. "You'll see. Don't look like that." She picked up a cookie from the plate and put it down again. "Store-bought." She sniffed. "I'll make you some real ones tomorrow."

Meg tried to smile. Imagine thinking about baking cookies after being shouted at like that! "I love your cookies," she said in a quavery voice. She hugged her grandmother again. "I'll change my bed and clear out a drawer for your things."

At the sight of the suitcase in the hall she turned back to the old lady sitting at the table. "How did you happen to come today, Grandma?" she asked. "Did Mama call you and tell you Dad went away?"

"Oh, no." For the first time, her grandmother looked uncomfortable. "I just knew."

"How could you know?" Meg waited. "You mean you guessed he'd gone?"

Grandma Korshak glanced out the window and then back at Meg. "No, no," she muttered. "I didn't guess." She lowered her voice to a whisper. "If your mama asks, you mustn't tell her," she said. "She wouldn't like me to say it, but it's true. I had a dream last night."

71

CHAPTER 8

Bill's Bombshell

Meg woke late, a little cramped from her night on the living-room sofa, and excited without knowing why. She sat up. Dad? She pushed the thought of him away. Linda's party? Yes, this was the day. But there was something else to think about, something more important than the party.

She sniffed. A syrupy smell—what was that? Then she knew. Grandma Korshak was in the kitchen making her special paper-thin pancakes, warming the maple syrup, spooning her homemade jam and boysenberry sauce into little dishes. Grandma Korshak—who had dreams that came true. That was it—that was what was making Meg's stomach do flip-flops this Saturday morning. Grandma had dreamed that Meg's father was going away, and he had gone. She had packed her suitcase and come at once, because she knew her dream was a "real" one.

Grandma is a wonderful, normal person, Meg thought. *And if she isn't crazy, then I'm not either.* She felt as if a weight had been lifted from her mind, or at least made lighter.

She ran down the hall to her bedroom and scrambled through her closet for jeans and a clean shirt. There were a dozen questions she wanted to ask Grandma today. Did many of her dreams come true? Did she ever have dreams she couldn't understand? Had she had the dreams when she was a little girl? Bill had come home early the night before, and there had been no more chance to talk privately with Grandma.

Meg frowned, remembering how strangely her brother had acted. He had little to say, but he wanted to be with Grandma and Meg, anyway. Meg waited impatiently for him to tell Grandma his great news about the scholarship, but when she tried to tell it herself, he shook his head at her sharply.

Eventually her mother had come out of her bedroom to fix dinner. Her hair was combed and her nose powdered, and she smiled determinedly when she came into the kitchen.

"Telling your grandmother the good news?" she'd

asked at once, so Bill had had to talk about it. But how briefly, almost disinterestedly, he had described the contest and the award! Meg's frown deepened as she brushed her hair back behind her ears. Bill must have been terribly depressed all day, as she had been, thinking about her father on the Marquette bus. Maybe he wasn't able to feel good about anything right now.

Out in the kitchen, her grandmother scurried around like a dark, contented elf in the morning sunshine.

"You're hungry, I can tell," she announced as soon as she saw Meg. "Sit down and eat. We have enough pancakes to feed a big crowd, so you have to be *very* hungry."

She motioned toward the table where the others were already eating. Bill looked solemn, but he ate busily; no one could resist Grandma Korshak's pancakes. Their mother sat like a child, her feet close together, her face weary but not particularly sad. Meg felt a wave of love for her grandmother who, with her gentle ways and expert cooking, could make them all feel safe and cared for, at least for a while.

She sat down and let Grandma stack several pancakes on her plate. "One for strawberries, two for boysenberries—" Meg chanted.

"—and three for maple syrup," Grandma finished. It was their private joke, going back as far as Meg could remember.

She wondered what her father was having for breakfast in Marquette.

"What're you doing today, Ma?" Bill asked abruptly.

"Your grandmother and I are going downtown to look for shoes. We both need them." A glance passed between the two women, and Meg knew her mother was sorry for the way she had spoken the night before. She wouldn't say so, but Grandma Korshak understood.

"I'm going to get ready for the party," Meg offered. "Wash my hair, iron my yellow pajamas. Stuff like that."

"What party?" Her mother seemed startled. "What are you talking about?"

Meg looked at her. "Don't you remember—when Gracie came home with me after school to ask if I could go?" She should have guessed that her mother hadn't been thinking about anything but the quarrel. What if she said no to the party now?

"Linda Bell's slumber party," Meg said. "Her mother sent you a note, and you read it right here in this kitchen."

"No need to take that tone." Her mother shrugged. "I suppose it's all right. As long as you're properly chaperoned."

"Since Mrs. Bell wrote the note I'm sure—"

"All *right*." Her mother turned to Bill. "And you'll be at the Superette all day, as usual?"

"Almost as usual." Bill scooped up a last bite of pancake and strawberry jam. "I'm taking off a little early to see about a new job, Ma. There's an opening for a clerk at Thompson's Auto Supply, and I want to try for it."

"Do they need someone just for the summer? You'll have to tell them you'll be leaving to go to the university in September."

Bill took a deep breath. "The thing is," he said, "I've changed my mind about going on to school right now. I mean, I'd rather get a job, and see how things go. No big deal," he added hastily, as their mother gave a little gasp of dismay. "I talked to my adviser yesterday and told him I didn't think I'd be using the scholarship. It's nice—I'm proud to have won it and all that—but a scholarship isn't the biggest thing that ever happened."

The world stopped right then. Grandma sank into a chair and stared at Bill. Meg's mother looked dazed.

"You're kidding," Meg said. "You have to be."

Bill glared at her. "I'm not kidding. I've been thinking about it ever since—for a couple of days. We're going to need more money coming in around here. When Dad was home, there was always the chance he might get a regular job. But now—" He looked at his mother. "Don't cry, Ma. It's not that important."

"Not important?" His mother wiped her eyes. "It's *everything!* How can you say it's not important?"

Bill pushed back his chair and stood up. "I have to get to work," he said. "Let's talk about it later. Great pancakes, Grandma." He bent and kissed their mother on the top of her head, then hurried out.

"He'll get over this idea," Grandma Korshak said. "He's a good boy, and he wants to do the right thing. Just give him time to think it out."

"But if he turns down the scholarship"— Meg's mother was horrified—"they'll give it to someone else. This is the only chance he'll have!"

Grandma reached for the coffeepot and refilled the cups. "Just give him time," she said again. "It'll be all right."

"Do you really believe that?"

Grandma nodded, but she looked worried. Bill was stubborn. If he believed his help was needed at home, he would turn down the scholarship, and no one would be able to stop him. *Wait'll Dad hears that,* Meg thought. *Maybe writing is his life, but he's going to feel awful if Bill doesn't go to college.*

The breakfast dishes were washed and her mother and Grandma Korshak had left on their shopping trip before Meg remembered the questions she'd wanted to ask her grandmother. *I have to talk to her alone,* she thought. *I just have to.*

Gracie called four times while Meg was washing her hair, packing her overnight bag, and doing her regular Saturday housekeeping chores.

"It's going to be so much fun!" Gracie said, sighing. "I just can't wait till tonight."

Meg felt the same way, but not for the same reason. Her mother and grandmother came home around noon, and the three of them had a strained and silent lunch. Afterward, Grandma said she was going to take a nap. There were dark circles under her eyes, and she shuffled as she went down the hall to the bedroom.

Grandma says everything is going to be all right, but she's really scared, just like we are, Meg thought. As much as she wanted a private talk with her grandmother, she realized it would have to wait.

At six o'clock, Bill hadn't returned. It was nearly time for Meg to meet Gracie.

"Your grandmother and I will have our dinner when he comes." Meg's mother lifted a casserole from the oven and spooned a generous helping onto a plate. "Eat," she ordered. "If this slumber party is like the ones I used to go to, you'll be up all night stuffing yourselves with nothing but junk food." She looked at Meg with a wistful expression. "It was fun," she said. "I'm glad you're going."

Brookfield Avenue was hushed and silvery when Meg stepped out into the warm evening. She was surprised to see Bill on the steps, his dark head next to Rhoda's auburn one. Neither of them had heard her coming.

"You'll be sorry," Rhoda was saying. "I don't mean just because you'll lose the scholarship. That's bad enough, but you'll be sorry because it's a really dumb thing to do. Take my word for it."

Meg cleared her throat. "Mama and Grandma are waiting for you upstairs," she said, trying not to sound as if she were butting in. "Did you get the job at the auto-supply store?"

Bill stood up. "I won't know till next week," he said shortly. "I'd better go up. Mustn't keep the ladies waiting."

"Listen." Rhoda put up a hand. "I've got a thing to tell you. It'll just take a minute."

Bill glanced at Meg then, and winked. "Yes, ma'am," he said and sat down on the steps again. "Tell away, ma'am."

Rhoda ignored his teasing tone. "It's about what I did when my mother moved to Los Angeles," she said. "That was the worst time in my life. I didn't know how to act. At first I cried and moped around, and then I got mad. I decided to get even with my mother for dropping out of our family."

"How?" Bill looked interested.

"I dropped out, too. I quit school."

"You couldn't do that," Meg protested. "People can't just quit because they feel like it."

Rhoda went on as if she hadn't heard. "Every morning I left when my father did and went to the zoo or to a movie. Or I just wandered around the shopping center near our house. I did that for nearly two weeks." She paused, remembering what it was like.

"So what happened?" Bill asked.

"So the school kept calling my father, and I kept telling him there was some mix-up in the office. Finally they convinced him that I wasn't in school and they wanted to know what was going on. And after that he took me right to the school door every morning before he went to work. Like a prisoner! But there was a counselor—"Rhoda hunched forward, and her husky voice softened—"a really neat person. We talked every day, and once she said, 'Tell me what you thought about when you weren't coming to school.' I told her I thought about how lonely I was, and about how far behind I was getting in all my classes. She said, 'That doesn't sound like much fun. What else did you think about?' And I told her I thought about how rotten my mother would feel if she knew her only child was walking around a shopping center instead of going to school. But, of course, my mother didn't know anything about it. And the counselor said it sounded like a pretty boring couple of weeks. And all of a sudden

I knew she was right. Quitting school wasn't what *I* wanted at all. The only person feeling rotten was little old Rhoda."

She leaned back and looked at Bill with an elfin grin. "That's all," she said. "You'd better eat now."

"Interesting story," Bill said. He stood up and turned to go inside, almost bumping into Meg.

"Have a good time at the party," he said, and Rhoda repeated the words as Meg brushed past them both.

"I will," she replied, with more force than was really necessary. She hurried toward the corner without looking back. It was pretty irritating to realize that Rhoda Deel might understand Bill and influence him, when he wouldn't listen to his own family.

Boys! she thought. And then, remembering the thoughtful expression on her brother's face, she decided she couldn't be jealous of Rhoda. She was a smart girl. And after all, it really didn't matter who said the right words to Bill, as long as he heard them.

CHAPTER 9

Linda's Party

Linda Bell's house was dark gray with white shutters, a rambling picture book house partly hidden by a row of precisely trimmed shrubs. A narrow drive curved up to the door and framed a bed of yellow tulips. Tall birches stood at either side of the drive.

"Isn't it beautiful?" Gracie said solemnly. "Don't you just love it?"

"I love it." Meg wondered if anything bad could happen to people who lived in a house like this one. Surely the children would be beautiful (Linda was beautiful) and the father would love his family and never want to leave them. No one would argue. The mother would be happy. Meg imagined herself and her family living here, serene and happy. Rich.

"We must be the first ones to come," Meg said. "There aren't any lights."

The door opened before Gracie could reply. Linda ignored their shy hellos.

"Can you believe it—the darned stereo isn't working right!" she stormed. "I just knew something like this would happen! It always does!"

Well, maybe little things could go wrong, even in this house, Meg thought. They followed their hostess into the foyer and toward a stairway that floated upward in a graceful curve.

"Take your stuff upstairs," Linda ordered. "Any bedroom where the door's open. I have to go back and see if the guys can get the stupid stereo going. It's making a noise like a jet plane, but Ricky thinks he knows what's wrong. He'd better! My folks will kill me if they come home and find it broken."

She darted across the dark living room and out of sight. Meg and Gracie went upstairs, letting their hands slide over the silky-smooth banister.

"Linda says at Christmastime they pin their greeting cards on a wide red ribbon and let it hang from the second floor all the way down to the floor in the foyer," Gracie said. She was talking fast, as if she wanted to keep Meg from saying anything. "And they wind real holly around the banister."

At the top of the stairs was a carpeted hall with doors on either side, some opened, some closed. The girls peeked into each of the opened ones. Knapsacks and overnight cases were dropped on some of the beds. The rooms were beautiful, and each of them was at least twice as big as Meg's bedroom at home.

"This'll be okay." Gracie turned into the last room on the left and dropped her bag on the twin bed nearest the door. "Let's go," she said. "The party's down in the rec room. Hurry up, Meggie."

Meg found her voice at last. "Where are Linda's mother and dad?" she asked. "I thought you said they'd be home."

Gracie grabbed Meg's hand and pulled her toward the hall. "Maybe they had to go out somewhere," she said impatiently. "What difference does it make?"

"Well, it just seems kind of strange. . . ." Meg needed time to think. "This is a pretty room, isn't it?" she said lamely. "I wouldn't mind having it, would you?" She looked at the braided rug, the white chenille bedspreads, the full, ruffled curtains. There was a worn teddy bear in a rocking chair near a window.

"Yes, it's a pretty room." Gracie ground out the words between clenched teeth. "Come on, Meggie! What's the matter with you? Don't you know how lucky we are to be here?"

There was no way Meg could explain the uneasiness

she felt at the news that Linda's parents had gone out. Reluctantly, she followed her friend down the wide, curving stairs.

"That's Mr. Bell's study," Gracie said, pointing through a dark doorway. "The family room's back there." She crossed the living room and hurried through the arch where Linda had disappeared earlier. Electric candles glowed in wall brackets. "This is the dining room—obviously. Just look at all the silver in that cabinet! And this is the door to the basement. Wait'll you see the rec room!"

Meg stopped Gracie as she was about to open the basement door. "Don't you think it's *funny* that Linda's folks aren't home? If I had a beautiful house like this, I'd stay around. I mean, something could happen—the stereo's broken already."

"Oh, for pete's sake!" Gracie sounded genuinely angry. "If you really want to know, they don't even know about this party. They've gone to a wedding in Chicago, and they won't be home until tomorrow afternoon. You and I are going to help Linda clean up after everyone else leaves."

"The note from Mrs. Bell—?" But Meg had already guessed the answer to her question. "Did you type it?"

"Linda did. I told her my mother and your mother would expect a letter or a phone call or something. Look, Meggie . . ." She changed to a let's-be-sensible voice. "What're you getting so upset about? Linda's folks wouldn't care about the party if they did know. They want her to enjoy herself. We're not babies— we're not going to hurt anything. And we're going to have a great time. Beginning now!"

She flung open the door and started down the stairs. Meg followed, not knowing what else to do. But as she looked over Gracie's shoulder, her uneasiness turned to panic. Blue light welled up from below, a murky blue that made her feel as if she were descending into a bottomless cave.

"Wait—" she began, but Gracie interrupted.

"Listen to that crazy stereo. It sounds like music from the moon!"

Meg clung to the railing. There was no music, just a furious, throbbing hum. Whatever was wrong with the stereo was magnified a hundred times by the loudspeakers. Meg shuddered. She'd heard the sound before. The nightmare "real" dream of a couple of nights ago was waiting at the foot of the stairs.

Numbly she trailed after Gracie. A sweetish fragrance filled her nostrils. It seemed to be a part of the smoky blue light that came from recessed lamps in the ceiling. Across the room, a group of boys huddled over the stereo, laughing loudly at the sounds the machine was making. Linda was with them, a paper cup in her hand. Three or four couples shuffled slowly around the room, their hands on each other's shoulders or at their sides, swaying to a beat of their own.

Another group was gathered around a corner table that held an array of bottles.

Meg didn't recognize anyone. Most of the boys were tall—much taller than the boys in Linda's eighth-grade class.

"What's that smell?" she whispered, trying to keep her voice steady. "It's grass, isn't it? Somebody's smoking grass! Oh, Gracie!"

But Gracie was halfway across the room, calling to Linda.

Meg felt as if she were frozen where she stood. Something terrible was going to happen. She knew it, just as she had known it in her dream. The blue light and the throbbing hum were no longer a mystery, but the fear was just as real, and the certainty that she must get away. She took a step and stumbled.

"Watch it, clumsy."

Meg looked down. She had tripped over someone's bare foot. A boy and girl lay in each other's arms, sharing a cigarette and grinning up at her. "If you broke my toe, I'll kill you," the girl murmured lazily.

Meg staggered backward. Any moment now the terrible thing would happen, the thing that came after the light and the sound and the bare foot in the dream. She gave a strangled cry and stumbled up the stairs.

"Meg!" It was Gracie. "Where're you going?"

Meg looked back and saw her friend with a boy across the room. In the blue light, Gracie's face was like a mask, her lipstick a dark streak. She could have been a stranger.

Meg shook her head and kept on going. How could she explain this feeling of dread? What could she say that Gracie would understand? It was no use trying.

The door at the top of the stairs was open. Meg slammed it behind her and leaned against it, shutting herself off from the party. But the panic was still there. Sobbing, she ran through the living room and out into the foyer. The big front door stuck when she tugged it, and she thought she was going to be sick right there in the Bells' front hall. Then the door swung open, and with a soft wail Meg ran out into the June night.

CHAPTER 10

Giggles and Buried Treasure

With trembling fingers Meg dug a half-dollar from her wallet and dropped it into the fare box of the crosstown bus. The first seat was empty, and she sank into it with a sigh.

"What's the matter, kid? Somebody after you?" The bus driver watched her in his mirror.

Meg shook her head. "I just felt like running," she puffed.

She had, in fact, run the two blocks from Linda's house to the bus stop as if a horde of devils were chasing her. And with every step she'd felt better. When she reached the corner and saw the lights of the bus a half-block away, she had almost laughed out loud. *I made it,* she thought. *I got away.* From what? She didn't know. But the panic was gone. It had started to fade as soon as the Bells' front door closed behind her.

"You shouldn't be out on the street by yourself at night," the bus driver muttered. He had a nice face—a fatherly face, Meg thought with a pang. "You're askin' for trouble."

"It was—a kind of emergency." Meg closed her eyes to end the conversation, leaning back to enjoy this feeling of relief. She needed time to think. In a few minutes she'd be home, and what would she tell her mother?

I could say I left the party when I found out Linda's folks weren't home. Or when I smelled marijuana. Or when I saw that all the other kids were a lot older than Gracie and I, Meg thought. But she didn't want to be a tattletale or sound like a goody-goody. The truth was that if it hadn't been for the dream, she would still be at the party. She wouldn't have smoked grass or done anything else she didn't want to do. But she would have stayed. As Gracie had said, she wasn't a baby.

I'll have to say I just wasn't having any fun, so I decided to leave. Her mother wouldn't be satisfied with that explanation—particularly when Meg came in without her overnight case—but it would have to do.

And what about Gracie? If something terrible was going to happen at the party, Gracie would be right in the middle of it. Yet there was no way Meg could have persuaded her friend to leave, even if she had tried. Gracie would have made fun of the "real" dream. She would have called Meg crazy.

Meg thought longingly of Grandma Korshak, who'd be sitting in front of the television set right now, watching Lawrence Welk and humming under her breath. *She's not crazy, so I'm not crazy. I think.* If only there had been a chance to talk with Grandma before the party!

"Brookfield Avenue."

The bus driver shook his head when Meg stood up.

"Someone should be meeting you at the corner," he scolded, peering into the dark. "Do you have far to go?"

"Just a block," Meg said. "I'll be okay. Thanks."

When the bus pulled away, she walked with dragging steps past the Superette and along the sidewalk where Bill had whirled in endless cartwheels just a few short days before. She looked up at the windows of her apartment. Most of the building was dark, but there was a soft light in the Korshaks' living room. The Deels' second-floor apartment was lighted, too. As Meg looked, Rhoda passed a window and glanced out.

Rhoda! Meg walked faster. Rhoda wouldn't mind an unexpected caller on her first Saturday night in a new city. She'd be pleased. They could talk for a while, and Meg could put off facing her mother.

She began to run toward the light.

Rhoda's welcoming smile almost split her small, freckled face.

"What happened to the slumber party?" she demanded. Then, without waiting for a reply, she turned and led the way to the kitchen. "Boy, am I glad to see you! This was turning out to be the longest evening in the history of the world. My dad's gone out, and I've read everything in the house. Now I'm making buried treasure. Want some?"

"Sure. Whatever buried treasure is." Meg looked around the kitchen. It was like the Korshaks' but with interesting differences. Half the table was taken up with African violets—sturdy clusters of pink, purple, lavender, and white. Brightly enameled tins stood in a row on the counter, and there were cheerful paintings on the walls and even on the ends of the cupboards.

"The paintings are my dad's," Rhoda said. "For a while he stayed home and painted every night. Now he goes out. The violets are mine. Look at that white one in the middle. It's fifteen inches across."

Meg looked and admired, then joined Rhoda at the sink where she was preparing the buried treasure.

"What you do," Rhoda explained, "is peel a couple of bananas and push them down into a bowl of halfway melted ice cream—like this. And then you push in some peanuts—like this. And then some cherries. And then"—she opened the freezer door and popped the big bowl inside—"you wait. When the ice cream is hard again, you pour about a gallon of fudge sauce over the whole thing. It's terrific! I made up the recipe myself. I figured it out once when my dad brought home some ice cream and put it into the refrigerator instead of the freezer."

"How long will it take to get hard?" Meg discovered that she was starving. So much had happened since she'd eaten.

"Not long. Not long at all, if you don't mind mushy ice cream."

Rhoda waved her into the living room and settled into a rocking chair. "Now tell me," she said. "Why aren't you at the party?"

There was something about Rhoda that made talking easy. Meg understood why Bill had confided in her about his decision to give up the scholarship. Rhoda looked—Meg puzzled over the right word—she looked more than interested. She looked as if she cared.

"I just wasn't having any fun," Meg said, because that was what she had planned to say at home. But then the rest of the story spilled out. She told Rhoda about the marijuana and the note that Linda had written and the feeling that something terrible was going to happen. She told her how much she dreaded tomorrow, when Gracie would call in a rage because Meg had run off without an explanation. She confided everything except the part about the "real" dream.

"And so that's why I came home," she finished. "Tomorrow Gracie will probably say it was the best party she ever went to, but I don't care. I'm just worried about what to tell my mother. If she knew all the stuff I've told you, she'd never let me go anywhere with Gracie again."

"I think you were smart to leave," Rhoda said, her thin face solemn. "And I'm really glad you're here. Why don't you stay with us tonight? I have twin beds in my room. My dad won't care—he probably won't even know. We can have a slumber party of our own."

The rest of the evening was the way a slumber party should be—lots of talk, lots of giggling, popcorn popped in a frying pan, cocoa with marshmallows on top, and the buried treasure that was just as delicious as Rhoda had promised it would be.

Rhoda talked about the friends she'd left in New York and about the summer after her mother left, when her father had sent her to a camp in Connecticut. "The thing is, I'm not the camp type," she said. "I don't like to swim or paddle a canoe or make beady things. I like to read and figure out science experiments and go to movies and play chess. The only time I had any fun was when we played softball. After two weeks, my dad came to visit me, and I told him I wanted to go home. He said I couldn't. I had to learn to be adaptable, if I was having a bad time. So we said good-by, and while he was talking to my counselor, I hid in the back of our van. He didn't know I was there until we were back in Manhattan, and then it was too late."

"Was he angry?"

"Was he!" Rhoda chuckled. "But after a while he started to laugh. Then he called the camp and told them to send my things home, and I never had to go there again."

"Bill went to camp once," Meg said. "He didn't like it much either." *My brother and Rhoda are a lot alike,* she thought.

At twelve o'clock they switched on television and watched the Midnight Horror Show. At two o'clock they went to bed. Even after the lights were out, they kept on talking, sharing every funny, sad, or silly thing they could think of.

Finally Rhoda's voice cracked, and she gave up. "Good night, Meg."

"Good night." With a contented sigh, Meg closed her eyes. *Funny world,* she thought. A terrible evening had changed into a terrific one.

But a moment later she was sitting up in bed, staring into the darkness. Behind her eyelids the blue light had been waiting, and the ominous hum of the stereo in Linda's rec room. The fear was there, too. With Rhoda's help she had banished it for a while, but it hadn't really gone away.

For the rest of the night, Meg tossed and turned while the blue light flickered around her. She shouldn't have left the party. She was glad she had. If she'd stayed, she would have had a good time. If she'd stayed, she would have been sorry. *I'm strange, creepy, crazy,* she thought, just before she finally went to sleep. That was what Gracie and Linda would say—and, yes, maybe even Rhoda, too—if they knew the truth.

CHAPTER 11

The Secret Window

Meg opened her eyes to sunshine and the sound of church bells. When had she finally dozed off? It seemed just a few minutes ago. Now she was fully awake, churning with thoughts of the night before and of what the day might bring. There would be an angry phone call from Gracie. She jumped out of bed. It would be terrible if her mother answered the phone and found out that Meg had left the party.

In the other bed, Rhoda slept soundly. One arm hung over the side, and the other was flung across her eyes. The sheets were tangled around her like the wrappings of a mummy.

As quietly as possible, Meg dressed. The bedroom

door across the hall was closed; Rhoda's father must have come in very late. Meg decided to wait until she got upstairs to use the bathroom. She went out to the kitchen and found a notepad and a pencil next to the telephone. *Good slumber party,* she wrote. *See you later. Thanks for letting me stay.* She moved one of the African violets to the edge of the table and propped the note where Rhoda couldn't miss it.

The apartment corridors were quiet, with fat Sunday papers lying in front of most of the doors. Meg hurried upstairs and picked up the paper at the Korshaks' door. She took a deep breath, slipped her key into the lock, and tiptoed inside.

The apartment was full of life. Grandma Korshak was an early riser, and Meg's mother was, too. A radio played hymns in the kitchen, and the shower roared in the bathroom. Meg tiptoed down the hall to her bedroom. Only Bill's door was still closed.

Swiftly she combed her hair into its usual single glossy braid. She rubbed her cheeks to give them color and ran her tongue over her teeth. *Okay so far,* she thought. As long as no one had seen her come in, there wouldn't be questions about her missing overnight case. She wondered how she'd get it back. Maybe Gracie would bring it over, but she doubted it.

Grandma was in the kitchen, humming "Onward, Christian Soldiers" along with the radio choir and poking at the bacon on the stove.

"Meggie!" She pattered across the linoleum and gave Meg a hug. "I didn't think I'd see you before I went home. Your mama said girls stay up and talk all night at these parties, so you'd probably sleep until noon. How is it you're home?"

"I just didn't want to stay any longer." Meg hurried to change the subject. "When are you leaving, Grandma? I have to talk to you before you go."

The bacon sputtered, and her grandmother rushed back to the stove. "I go right after lunch," she said. "There's a bus to Waukesha at two thirty. But first, we go to church together, your mama and Bill and me. And then we go to a restaurant for lunch. My treat." Her smile slid away for just a moment. "I want us to do something together—a family, see?—before I go. Now you'll come with us, huh?"

"Oh, yes." Meg hadn't been to church for a long time. She was glad to go, particularly since she'd be there with her grandmother.

"And after lunch you take me to the bus station," Grandma went on. "Just you."

Breakfast passed without more questions, except for Bill asking Meg if she'd had a good time last night. "Yes," Meg replied uncomfortably. She resolved to tell Bill later that she hadn't stayed at Linda's party.

Meg's mother said nothing. She seemed to have left them just as Meg's father had. In her place was a quiet stranger who seemed always to be thinking of other things. It was Grandma Korshak who reminded Meg not to dawdle over her bacon and eggs and asked her if she had a dress ready to wear to church.

The white walls and tall stained-glass windows of the church offered a special welcome that morning. Meg sat between her mother and her grandmother and let the organ music wash over her. She felt serene for the moment, as if her problems couldn't follow her here. She hoped her mother felt the same way.

"Nice windows." Grandma's face was rosy in the reflected light. "The middle one is the best."

Meg followed her grandmother's gaze. A golden ladder stretched upward against blue glass sky. At its top, a cluster of angels hovered.

"Jacob's ladder," Grandma whispered. "He dreamed that he saw a ladder going up to heaven. God spoke to him from the top of the ladder and said the land where he was sleeping was his to keep. Wasn't that a wonderful thing?"

Meg looked at Grandma sharply. Was it the beauty of the design that pleased her grandmother, or was it Jacob's dream? The sleeping figure at the foot of the ladder was somehow reassuring. Like the artists at the museum, Jacob had dreamed, and his life was better because of it.

The hymn singing was Meg's favorite part of the service. "When I fall on my knees, With my face to the rising sun, O Lord, have mercy on me." She sang

enthusiastically, blending her voice with a quavery so-
prano and a booming bass behind her. Later, when the
minister asked the congregation to put aside their sor-
rows and give thanks for their blessings, Meg felt as if
he were speaking directly to her. She thought of
Rhoda Deel's welcoming smile the night before. Of all
the millions of people who might have moved into the
empty second-floor apartment, Rhoda had come.
Wasn't that a kind of miracle?

She peeked at her family. Her mother's face had
tightened under the minister's suggestion to count her
blessings, but Bill and Grandma looked thoughtful.
Thank you for my family, Meg prayed. *Thank you for my
friends.* And then, *Please make my father sorry he went
away. Make Bill go to college. Don't ever let me have a "real"
dream again . . . at least, not the scary kind.*

After the service they walked to a cafeteria nearby,
where Grandma made scornful comments about the
soup and rolls, admitted the roast beef was pretty
good, and insisted they all have double-dip sundaes for
dessert. "You must come out to Waukesha soon," she
said as they left the restaurant. "I'll make bean soup
you won't forget."

When they returned to the apartment, Grandma
called Meg into the bedroom to help her with her
suitcase. "I told Bill you will go alone with me to the
bus station," she whispered. "Your mama wouldn't
want to go, anyway."

That was true; her mother had already said her good-bys and gone back to her bedroom. Meg darted down the hall to Bill's room and told him that if Gracie called he should say Meg would be back in a little while. Soon she and Grandma were out on the street again, with Meg carrying the suitcase. It was very light; her grandmother didn't need much but her nightgown and an extra dress. Most of the space had been taken up by the jars of preserves and boysenberry sauce she brought each time she came.

"Now," Grandma said, as soon as they were settled on the city bus, "what is it you want to talk about, Meggie? Your dad and your mama, I guess. But I don't know what's going to happen there. I'm so sorry for your mama. I don't like this thing your father's done."

"It's not that, Grandma," Meg said. "It's something else. I wanted to ask you about the dream you had. The one about Dad going away." Meg hesitated. Grandma was looking at her with a strange expression.

"I'm sort of interested in dreams," Meg went on cautiously. "Especially dreams that come true." She waited, but her grandmother didn't say anything. "What I want to know is, do you have them often?"

"Pretty often," Grandma said. "Why do you care about that?"

"I just wondered." *"Pretty often"—what did that mean?* "It seems funny," Meg continued. "I mean, you act as if it was just an ordinary thing. And it isn't!" Her voice rose in spite of herself. "It's kind of—kind of crazy."

She hadn't meant to use that word, but she couldn't help it. *Crazy* had been lying right there on her tongue, waiting to be spoken.

Her grandmother didn't seem to mind. "Not crazy," she said, with a little chuckle. "When I was a girl, I thought, yes, there is something wrong with me. I would stare in the mirror and think, you look like nothing much, and your clothes are like everybody else's, but inside you are different. Then I found out that my mama sometimes dreamed the truth, too. And she told me, 'We are lucky, you and I. We have a secret window to show us things.' I'd never thought of it as good luck. My older sister, she could sing like a lark, and my brother painted pictures, but I was the one with the secret window. It was my talent. My difference." Grandma looked at Meg shrewdly. "Don't you think a person is fortunate to have such a talent?"

Meg turned away. Grandma seemed to guess that she had "real" dreams, too, and wanted her to say she felt lucky. Well, she wouldn't. She wouldn't!

"Other people would laugh if you told them all that," she said bluntly. "You'd better not tell anyone else."

Grandma nodded. "I don't talk about it much. But I use my talent when I can. Like now. When I had the dream about your father going away, I knew you'd be unhappy, so I came. I wanted to be with you for a little bit."

Meg thought about the pancake breakfast on Saturday, the shopping trip with Mom, the hour at church, the cafeteria dinner—all the things Grandma had arranged to help them through this painful weekend. Because of the dream, she'd been there to take charge when they needed her most.

"We've always had artists and writers—talented people—in our family," Grandma continued. "I was proud of my brother and my sister, and I'm proud of your father's gift, too. I didn't want him to leave his family—that's a bad thing—but I want him to be a good writer. We can't choose the things that make us special, but we must use what we have."

"I don't care what *he* does," Meg said fiercely. "I'm sorry, Grandma, but I hate him."

Her grandmother patted her hand. "People with special gifts can be hard to live with," she said. "My brother, my sister. Your father. Your grandfather used to say I wasn't so easy to get along with either." She looked somber. "Your mama never wanted to hear about my dreams. She's had a hard life, Meggie, and she doesn't like things she doesn't understand. You know, I think she's been afraid for a long time that your father might leave. Perhaps if she hadn't been so afraid . . ."

"It wasn't Mama's fault," Meg said. But she wondered if Grandma might be right. If her mother hadn't forced a decision, maybe things would have gone on as they were until Dad decided for himself whether he was going to be a successful writer.

She brushed the thought away. No one had made him leave. *Writing is my life,* was what he'd said, and the next day he was gone. He was different from other fathers, all right, and the difference was terrible.

"Here's our stop." Meg tugged Grandma's suitcase from under the seat and helped her down the steps of the bus. "Thanks for telling me about your dreams, Grandma. I'm really glad you came to see us."

Grandma gave Meg a fierce hug. "You're a good girl, Meggie," she said. "Is there anything else you want to ask me?"

There was. "About the dreams," Meg said. "Do you ever get scared? What if you have a dream that's scary —a real nightmare? What if it makes you do something stupid?" She was thinking about how she'd run from Linda Bell's house.

Grandma hugged her again. "If that happens, I just wait," she said softly. "After a while, it nearly always comes clear. No good to worry. We have to be glad for what we know and what we have."

Minutes later, with her grandmother on the intercity bus for Waukesha, Meg thought about those words. *Be glad for what you know and what you have. . . .* A new friend, for instance, and a brother, a mother, a grandmother.

A secret window.

Would she ever be grateful for her "real" dreams? She doubted it! Looking into the future was just a family trait that she wished had ended with her grandmother.

CHAPTER 12

Bad News from Gracie

"Hey, what happened at that party last night?" Bill was curled up on the couch in the living room, a book balanced on his knees, a half-dozen others on the floor within arm's reach. "I thought you said you had a good time."

"What do you mean?" Meg looked over her shoulder. She hoped her mother was still lying down. "Did Gracie call me?"

"She sure did. She wants you to meet her at Darys' to talk about the party. And she didn't sound as if she was looking for a giggle-and-gossip session, either. She sounded M-A-D!" He grinned at her over his book. "Need a bodyguard? My rates are reasonable."

"No, thanks." Meg tried to smile and failed. Gracie must be really angry.

"I'll be back in a little while. Don't tell Mama Gracie was mad, okay?"

Bill nodded. "If you aren't home by suppertime, I'll call Gracie and ask where she's hidden the body." He went back to his reading, and Meg hurried out of the apartment. Sometimes Bill went too far with his so-called humor. But she knew it wasn't his teasing that made her so jumpy. It was the thought of facing her friend.

Gracie was waiting in front of Darys' Drugstore. Her arms were folded over her chest, her face was pale, and her whole body was rigid with anger.

"You fink!" She hurled the words across the sidewalk as Meg drew near. "I bet you really feel great about what you did!"

Meg stepped backward. "Now wait—" she began, then tried again. "I'm sorry I ran away last night. It was just—just a feeling I had that I shouldn't stay. Did you have fun?"

"Fun!" Gracie's voice cracked on the word, just as the door of the drugstore opened and Mr. Dary came outside and stretched. "Nice day," he said pleasantly. "Doesn't that sun feel good, girls?"

"Yes, it does," Meg murmured, her eyes on Gracie's face.

"Let's walk," Gracie said rudely. "I want to talk to

you in private, Meg." She started down the street, and Meg, with a quivery smile at Mr. Dary, hurried after her.

"What's wrong, Gracie? Did something happen at the party after I left?" She held her breath.

Gracie strode on, arms swinging, hands clenched in tight fists. "Did something happen?" she repeated. "As if you don't know! I didn't think you were a snitch, Meg Korshak, but I was wrong. Boy, was I wrong! Now I know what kind of person you are, and I'll never forgive you for what you did. Never!"

"But what did I do? I didn't want to stay at the party, so I came home. That's all. I knew you wouldn't like it, but I didn't think you'd care this much. I had this funny feeling that I didn't belong there."

They'd reached the corner, where an empty concrete bench marked the bus stop. Gracie sat down with a thump, and Meg sat beside her.

"Well, you're right about one thing," Gracie said. She was suddenly close to tears. "You didn't belong there. You're a baby and a stool pigeon, and by tomorrow morning there won't be a single person in school who'll have anything to do with you. You'll see!"

"Gracie, will you just tell me what I did that was so terrible? Please?" Meg struggled to keep her own anger under control. "I don't know what you're talking about."

"Don't lie!" Tears streamed down Gracie's cheeks,

but she didn't seem to notice them. "You called the police and told them there was a wild party going on at Bells'. Don't say you didn't—it had to be you. It's all your fault that we had to go to the police station, and they called everybody's parents, and Linda and two of the boys are being charged with possession of marijuana. I just hope you're satisfied!"

"The police!" Meg gasped. "I didn't call the police. Why would I do that? I didn't call anybody. I just went back to our apartment building, and I stayed overnight with the girl downstairs. You know, Rhoda—"

"I don't care where *you* stayed." Gracie was sobbing. "*I* was in the police station. I was *searched.* My *mother* was called to the police station, and she's so mad she's ready to kill me. I'm grounded for *three* months. The only reason I'm here now is because she had to work an extra shift. If she finds out I left the house, she'll probably make it *six* months, but I don't care. I wanted to tell you face to face what I think of you." She hiccupped noisily.

Meg put out a hand, but Gracie snatched her arm away. "So now you know." She was still sobbing. "I hate you, and Linda hates you, and every single person at that party hates you. Everybody hates a fink! Linda's folks probably hate you, too, because one of the boys was drunk and tried to get away from the police, and he broke a beautiful vase in the living room." She rubbed her eyes. "You're so mean!"

"Gracie, I didn't." Meg was stunned, angry, hurt. "I wouldn't snitch. It wasn't any of my business if the kids were smoking. I wasn't even sure it was marijuana." She leaned forward, trying to make Gracie look at her. "I don't tattle. Did I tell anyone that you put Mrs. Cobbell's hat on that statue?"

Gracie shook her head irritably. "That was different. That was just a joke. And I told you I was sorry. This was much, much worse." She dug for a tissue in her shoulder bag. "If you didn't leave Linda's to call the police, why'd you go?" she demanded. "Tell me that."

"I did tell you. I had a feeling—"

"Hah!" Gracie jumped up. "You had a feeling! I don't want to talk to you anymore. Not ever! You've spoiled everything. Linda says she never should have invited a couple of *babies* to her party. She blames me for bringing you. If you want to know what I think, I think you were jealous because Linda liked me, and you wanted to make trouble. Well, you did. You've made lots of trouble! Fink!"

She was gone, stomping down the street, her dark hair bouncing on her shoulders. Meg was unable to move.

I'm going to pretend this didn't happen, she thought. But she couldn't forget the things Gracie had said. She shuddered when she thought about the police. If she'd stayed at the party, she'd have gone to the station with the others. She'd have been searched. Her mother would have been called. She pictured her mother, already so stiff and silent under the weight of her father's going. *I've come to get my daughter out of jail, officer. I want you to know that her older brother would never get into such trouble. The second child in our family was strictly an accident.*

"Coming or not, sister?"

Meg looked up. A bus had rolled up to the corner and the driver was looking at her through the open door.

"I'm sorry—I was just thinking." Meg got up hurriedly. The driver slammed the door and drove off.

What a mess it all was!

As she started home, Meg was more confused than she'd ever been in her life. The dream about the blue light had saved her from a dreadful experience, that was true. Even though it was embarrassing to have run away from the party, it would have been worse to have stayed. Still, she couldn't tell anyone about the dream, so she was in trouble, anyway. *Who wants a talent if it makes everyone hate you?* she thought bitterly. *Who cares about having a secret window? I just want to be like everyone else.*

Then, as she turned the corner, a familiar figure crossed Brookfield Avenue. It was Rhoda, looking more like a skinny little boy than ever in her blue jeans, T-shirt, and a bright orange baseball cap. She had a Yo-Yo in her hand and was sailing it expertly ahead of her. Watching her, Meg felt better.

"Rhoda!" she shouted. "Wait a minute. I'll walk with you."

Rhoda turned and waved, and Meg began to run. All at once she felt light, as if with each long step the burden of Gracie's anger was left a little farther behind.

CHAPTER 13

A Long, Long Day

The dream was quick and terrifying. *Meg stood on a high place—a cliff—and looked down at glittering water. Far out from shore, a small red rowboat bobbed like a toy. One oar dangled in the water, the other floated away. The boat was empty. But someone she cared about had been in the boat just a minute before. As she stared, the water turned dark, and the boat began to move swiftly away.*

Meg screamed, a harsh, hurting sound that brought her mother rushing into the bedroom.

"Meg, what in the world!"

Meg struggled to sit up. Her throat ached with the sound she'd made.

"You must have had a nightmare," her mother said.

She sat on the edge of the bed. "You made a simply terrible sound—as if you were choking."

"I'm okay now." Meg longed to hurl herself into her mother's arms. Instead, she lay back on the pillows. "I'm fine."

"We're all having trouble sleeping, I guess." Her mother sighed and looked at Meg. "I'm sorry you have to go through all this," she said. "I'd like you and Bill to be happy all the time." She smoothed Meg's hair back from her face. "You probably think grown-ups understand their own feelings and have good reasons for what they do. I remember when I believed that. The truth is, we just do the best we can, from day to day, and lots of times everything goes wrong. Then we're unhappy, and our children are unhappy, too. And have nightmares." She shook her head. "What was it you dreamed?"

"Nothing important, Mama." Meg pretended to yawn. "Just silliness. I'm fine now."

Her mother sat for a minute longer, absentmindedly smoothing the bed covers. "Well, good night, then," she said at last. "You'll sleep all right now, won't you? I'll leave the lamp on if you want."

Meg waited until she heard her mother's door close behind her. Then she slipped out of bed and tiptoed to her bureau. She wouldn't sleep again until she wrote down the dream.

What could it mean? *Water,* she wrote, crouched

close to the open window. *A little red boat—nobody in it.* Whom did she know who might have been in the boat?

The answer was right there in Meg's head, as it had been from the moment she woke up. She shivered, in spite of the warm night. *Dad is at Lake Superior,* she wrote. *He's all alone up there.* She imagined her father on the shore of the great lake, pushing off in the red boat.

With a little moan she closed the notebook and pressed her forehead against the screen. In the quiet of the night she could almost hear her heart thumping. It had happened again, this sudden, unwanted look into the future. And what was she to do about it this time?

She switched off the lamp her mother had left on and went back to bed. There was nothing she could do tonight. She closed her eyes and willed herself to sleep, trying to ignore the insistent voice—the angry voice—that whispered in the darkness:

You don't have to do anything. No one asked him to go away and live by himself. Why should you worry? He isn't worrying about what happens to you.

It was raining when Meg woke the next morning, a hard splat of sound against the window her mother had closed some time during the night. Meg remembered the dream, and she saw again the darkening water and the helpless boat. She burrowed deeper under the sheet and tried to forget.

"Meg, get up." Her mother opened the bedroom door. "Someone's on the phone for you."

Reluctantly Meg pushed back the covers and went out to the kitchen. It was Rhoda calling. She sounded sleepy.

"I just wondered if you'd like me to walk to school with you. I mean, I don't have anything else to do this morning."

What a good friend Rhoda was! Yesterday afternoon she'd listened sympathetically to Meg's half-tearful story of her meeting with Gracie. And this morning she'd realized Meg would be dreading school.

"You don't have to," Meg said. "I'm okay. Thanks, anyway."

"I wish I was going to classes," Rhoda said. "I guess I could have, if I'd said I wanted to. It didn't seem worth it for just a few days. We could have eaten lunch together today."

"I wish you were, too," Meg said. "But, honestly, it's okay. I'll see you when I get home."

"Right. I guess I'll go to the branch library and apply for a card today." Rhoda paused as if searching for words. "Don't let any of those creeps make you feel bad," she said with sudden violence, and hung up.

The rain continued. Meg's mother made her carry an umbrella when she left the apartment. She tilted it against the wild, wet wind, while little umbrella islands bobbed past her.

The walk was too short. As Meg opened the big front door, something dropped with a crash at her feet. It was her overnight case. She closed her umbrella and discovered Linda Bell standing in front of her. Several girls and boys stood nearby, watching curiously.

"I don't want your crummy junk lying around my house." Linda's voice was low and shaking with anger. "From now on, you'd better keep out of my way, or you'll be sorry."

A trickle of rain wriggled down Meg's spine. She felt like a clammy mess next to Linda, who was beautiful even when she was having a tantrum.

"Why'd you do it?" Linda demanded. "Just tell me that one thing."

Meg picked up the overnight case and took a deep breath. "Gracie told me what happened," she said. "But if you believe I called the police, you're wrong. I'd never do that. I'm sorry about your party—thanks for bringing my overnight case."

She tried to walk away, but Linda moved in front of her. "I shouldn't have invited you." Her voice turned shrill. "I'll know better next time—if there ever is a next time! My mother and father got called home from their trip because of you, and I'm going to be grounded *forever* because of you. Nasty snitch!" She whirled around to the group gathered behind her.

"Let's get out of here," she snapped. "I don't like the atmosphere."

When they'd gone, Meg climbed the stairs to her locker on the second floor. Gracie's locker was next to hers, but Gracie had arrived early and was already hurrying down the hall to her first class. The sight of her friend running away hurt more than the scene with Linda. Gracie and Meg had gone to kindergarten together. They'd shared comic books, made scrapbooks of their favorite stars, traded clothes and secrets, spent long, lovely Saturday afternoons talking and dreaming about the things they'd do when they were older. Gracie was part of Meg's life. Losing her was like losing a sister.

Meg crammed the overnight case into her locker and took out the books she'd need for her first two classes. Was it her imagination, or was everyone looking at her disapprovingly as she made her way through the crowded corridors? By the time she reached her homeroom, she was sure she'd be an outcast forever.

It was a pleasant surprise to find her classmates laughing and to hear her name called as soon as she came through the door.

"Meg, over here. We're deciding what to take to the picnic tomorrow." Chris Svenson's face was glowing with enjoyment at being the center of a group. "I thought it'd be fun if we each brought a different kind of food and shared it. Do you want to go along, or would you rather bring your own lunch?"

The class picnic! Meg wondered if her life would ever be calm enough so she'd stop forgetting things. "I'll bring whatever you want," she said quickly. "That's a neat idea."

After more discussion, it was agreed that Meg and two other girls would make sandwiches for eight people. Chris offered to bake a cake, and the others would bring potato chips, pickles, carrot sticks, and apples. Soda and milk were to be provided by the school.

"Now don't anyone forget what you're supposed to bring," Chris ordered. She leaned across the aisle to Meg, just as Mrs. Cobbell rapped for order. "Want to sit with me on the bus tomorrow?" she whispered. "I'll save you a seat."

Meg nodded. Chris's invitation was the only sign that the other girls knew what had happened over the weekend. Before, Meg had always sat with Gracie on field trips.

The day seemed endless. Meg ate lunch with Chris, and Gracie sat across the room with another group. Gracie's friends giggled and looked over at Meg repeatedly, in a way that made her heart sink. By the time her last afternoon class ended, with Gracie sitting icily across the aisle, Meg could hardly wait to get home. It might not be the most cheerful place in the world, but no one hated her there.

A cheerful whistling greeted her as she opened the apartment door. Meg followed the sound to the kitchen and found Bill sitting at the table. He was looking with a pleased expression at the papers spread in front of him.

"Hi there." He leaned back, tipping his chair at a dangerous angle. "How was your day?—as if I had to ask."

"Awful," she told him.

"Gracie still mad?"

Meg nodded. Bill hadn't asked any questions last night when she came back from the meeting with Gracie. He waited now, but when Meg said nothing, he turned to another subject.

"I'm filling out my application for the university," he announced. "Next fall you can come to Madison and we'll take in a football game or two."

Meg forgot all about her bad day. "You've changed your mind about not going to school!" she exclaimed. "Oh, I'm so glad! Does Mama know? Was it what Rhoda said that made you decide?"

"I'll tell Ma tonight. And, yes, I guess it was Rhoda who got me thinking. She was right—I just wanted to get even with Dad for going away. I hate to admit it," he added teasingly, "but she's pretty smart for a little kid. And for a girl!"

Meg dropped in a chair and stuck out her tongue at

him. "We women are going to take over the world," she drawled. "You're going to need all the education you can get."

"Right." He was suddenly serious. "You know, all day yesterday I went over the whole thing in my mind —Dad leaving and how I felt about it. All that. It's a real pain, but I finally decided it isn't the end of the world. He has his life to live, I have mine. And I have better things to do with it than get even."

Meg listened intently. She wanted to understand this. She wanted to let Bill's words carry her up out of the gray world she'd been living in since their father left.

"But he shouldn't have gone," she protested. "How can you forgive him for that? I can't!"

Bill looked thoughtful. "I guess I can't either," he said. "But he's gone, and from now on that's going to be *his* problem, not mine."

"Do you still love him?" Meg asked. "Do you miss him?"

Bill's face tensed. "I can't stop loving him because he's done something dumb," he said slowly. "But I can't change what he's done, either."

Later, while Meg washed greens for salad and peeled potatoes, she thought about what Bill had said. From time to time she looked at him, hunched over the forms on the table. *He's a good person,* she thought. *Like Rhoda. Better than I am. I'm just full of meanness.*

That evening, when her homework was completed, she took out her box of stationery. She wrote quickly, before she could change her mind.

> *Dear Dad,*
>
> *Last night I dreamed about a little red rowboat in the water. It was empty, and one of the oars was floating away. I didn't actually see you in the dream, but I was pretty sure you'd been in the boat and had fallen out.*
>
> *Do you remember that time I dreamed about the burning house just before the Pancinos' Christmas tree caught fire? You said then I shouldn't talk about my dreams, so I never have. But I want you to know about this one. Sometimes my dreams do come true.*
>
> *Please be careful.*
>
> *Your daughter,*
Meg

Meg read it over carefully. It didn't sound especially friendly, but it wasn't unfriendly, either. She sighed. She couldn't be like Bill just by wishing it, but maybe the letter was a step in the right direction.

CHAPTER 14

Trouble at the Picnic

"Oh, Rhoda, that's terrific! When did you decide to go?"

Rhoda grinned at Meg. They'd met in front of the apartment, where Rhoda had been waiting, a wide straw hat in one hand and a brown paper bag in the other.

"Mr. Walsh—that's the adviser I talked to about my schedule for next year—called last night and asked if I wanted to go to the class picnic. He said it'd be a good chance to meet the kids before next fall, and he'd take me around and introduce me to everybody. At first I was going to say no—but then I thought, 'Why not?' " She cocked her head jauntily. "When I told him you and I lived in the same building, he said you could do the introducing instead of him. You don't have to do that, though," she added hastily. "I'll just tag along after you, okay?"

It was more than okay. Meg had never said more than a "Good morning" to Mr. Walsh, but he must be the best adviser in the entire school.

"If I'd known last night, I'd have told you not to bring lunch," she said excitedly. "We have the food all organized, and we're going to have twice as much as we need." The girls started up the block together. Looking around her as they walked, Meg noticed, for the first time, that it was a beautiful day, just right for a picnic.

When they reached the school grounds, buses were waiting to take the three seventh-grade homerooms to Westerbrook Park. Chris Svenson had saved seats in one of them for their group, and the girls easily made room for Rhoda.

"She's nice," Chris said softly, as the bus started up. "But when I saw you both coming across the school-yard, I thought, 'Meg must have a little brother I don't know about.' And then when you got closer, I saw the person walking with you was wearing those tiny gold earrings—"

"I'm going to be a late bloomer," Rhoda said, popping up over the seat in front of them. Chris ducked her head in embarrassment. "If I don't grow up to win the Nobel Prize in chemistry, I expect to be a sex symbol. Either way, you can say you knew me when." She joined in everyone's laughter, then sat back and asked the girl next to her about Westerbrook Park and what would be happening at the picnic. Meg knew she wouldn't have to spend much time introducing Rhoda to her classmates. By the end of the day she'd probably have talked to everyone, and everyone would like her.

As they pulled into the Westerbrook parking lot, Meg saw Gracie stepping down from the other bus. For a moment, they stared at each other through the dusty window. Gracie looked pale, and there was a dangerous glitter in her eyes.

"That's Gracie, right?" Rhoda was peering over the seat again. "Wow! Either she's still mad about the party or she *always* looks as if she's going to kill somebody. Which is it?"

"Come on, people—out of the bus!" Mrs. Cobbell saved Meg from having to answer. The girls gathered up their boxes, bags, and suntan lotion and hurried down the aisle. As they stepped out of the bus, a member of the Picnic Committee handed each of them a card.

"It's for the softball games," Meg explained. "Everybody gets to play." She looked at her card. "Game number one—girls against boys. Blue team."

"I'm blue, too," Rhoda said. "How's that for luck!"

The girls crossed the lawn to a table where Chris

collected the food they'd brought. "We're going to have a feast!" she gloated. "I wish we could eat right now."

"Tennis first," one of the girls said. "See you later." She hurried off toward the courts, just as a whistle sounded shrilly from the baseball diamond.

"That's for us," Meg said. "Game number one. Come on, Rhoda."

The teams organized quickly. Jean Monroe was named captain of the blue, and Meg found herself in line after Gracie in batting order. Jean came next, then Rhoda.

"Let's go, team!" The girls met Jean's shout with cheers, and the game began. The first batter struck out, and then it was Gracie's turn. She looked stiff and angry as she stalked to the plate, and the blue team grew silent. The first pitch was fast and low, and Gracie swung at it carelessly. Bat and ball connected in a solid hit.

"Run!" Jean screamed. Meg joined in the clapping as Gracie, jolted into action, raced to first base.

Meg was up next and struck out. Then Jean went to bat. She let two pitches go by and swung at the third. The looping ball went over the second baseman's head into center field, for a single. Gracie moved to third, and Rhoda picked up the bat.

It looked too long for her and too heavy.

"Join the Little League, kid!" one of the boys

shouted from the outfield. Rhoda didn't seem to hear him. Her face was calm, and a funny little smile tugged at her lips. There was something about the way she stood there, waiting for the pitch, that made Meg hold her breath.

Smack! The sound was like a small explosion. Some of the teachers turned to look, and the blue team screamed with joy. The ball streaked high and fast across the field and disappeared into the bushes beyond. Two fielders scrambled after it, while Gracie, Jean, and then Rhoda came flying into home.

They were met with cheers and hugs, and for just a moment Meg and Gracie were part of a shrieking tangle of players. Then Gracie pulled away and ran over to the sidelines.

The game continued, with Rhoda making another homer and driving in two more runs.

"Where did you learn to hit like that?" Meg demanded when the last inning ended and the teacher-umpire had announced the final score: Girls 9, Boys 7. Meg and Rhoda sat on a blanket under a maple tree and rubbed tanning lotion on their faces and arms.

"My dad was a Little League coach when we lived in New York." Rhoda kicked off her sneakers and wiggled her toes. "I never joined a team, but I used to sub once in a while, and my dad and I practiced together a lot. Back when I was a mere child," she added with dignity, and they both laughed.

Some of the picnickers produced Frisbees, and soon the air was full of flying saucers. Rhoda proved to be as skilled with a Frisbee as she was with a baseball bat, and the girls played until their legs gave out under them.

Promptly at noon Chris assumed her position as organizer of the feast. She spread a checked cloth on the table they had claimed and set her magnificent chocolate cake in its center. "Let's eat," she called, and soon the rest of the food was arranged in boxes and plastic bowls around the cake centerpiece.

Rhoda sat across from Meg. Her wide-brimmed straw hat was tipped far back on her head, and she ate with cheerful concentration.

"What kind of sandwich is that, Rhoda?" Chris asked. "It looks yummy. I'll trade you this ham-and-cheese for whatever it is."

Rhoda took another foil-wrapped packet from her lunch bag. "It's my own invention. Peanut butter, bologna, pickles, and just a tiny bit of horseradish—on pumpernickel," she said. "You'll love it."

Chris withdrew her outstretched hand. "I guess I'll stick with what I have."

"Anybody else want one? I brought plenty."

Rhoda just laughed when the other girls shuddered and refused. *Nothing bothers her,* Meg thought. *She is who she is, and she doesn't worry about things that aren't important, or things she can't change.* Meg remembered what Bill had said the night before. *I've got my life to live.* He and Rhoda liked other people, but they liked themselves, too. It was a good way to be.

Chris's cake was as delicious as it looked. Meg was finishing her second piece when she looked up and saw Gracie a few feet away, glowering. Jean Monroe was with her.

"Some people don't care whom they eat with." Gracie's voice was loud, meant to be heard. Silence fell over the group gathered around the table.

"I wouldn't eat lunch with a snitch if you paid me," Gracie continued. "You'd better be careful. If anybody says one little 'damn,' she'll run off and tell a teacher." Jean put out a protesting hand, but Gracie stepped away from her.

"Oh, for pete's sake." Chris wiped chocolate crumbs from her chin as she spoke. "If you're going to talk like that, go somewhere else, Gracie. We don't want to hear it."

Gracie whirled to attack. "Don't tell *me* what to do, Chris Svenson," she stormed. "You can be friends with a sneak if you want to, but just wait until she gets *you* into trouble. Then you'll be sorry."

When Meg opened her mouth to defend herself, no sound came out. The other girls looked down, embarrassed, or pretended to be busy packing up the remains of the lunch.

"Anybody want to go for a walk?" Rhoda asked. "I

have to work off all those terrific peanut butter and bologna sandwiches."

Gracie made a strangled sound. Her face was white with patches of red, and the cords in her throat were taut. Meg thought, *She's almost hysterical.*

"You may know how to bat a ball, but you don't know how to pick your friends," Gracie screamed at Rhoda. "Unless you *like* finky little tattletales!"

Jean grabbed Gracie's arm and tried to pull her away. "Come on, that's enough," she pleaded. "What's the use of calling names? It's not true, anyway. Meg didn't snitch about that party."

"She did!" Gracie looked betrayed. "She called the police."

"No, she didn't. Or if she did, she wasn't the only one. The Bells' neighbors called the police because the noise was keeping them awake. They thought the police would tell you to pipe down and that would be the end of it, but some of the kids were smoking grass. Linda's looking for someone to blame, but the whole thing's her own fault for having marijuana and liquor at the party. So why don't you just forget it?"

"You're lying!" Gracie shrieked. "You don't know anything about it!"

Jean looked frightened but determined. "I know because Mrs. Bell is in my mother's bridge club, and she told my mother last night that it was the neighbors who called the police. They knew Mr. and Mrs. Bell were away, and they were pretty sure Linda wasn't supposed to be having a party when they weren't home."

Gracie began to cry—breathless, childlike sobs that made Meg feel sorry for her in spite of the ugly things she'd said.

"I don't believe you," she wept. "Anyway, Meg Korshak, if you're not a snitch, you *are* crazy. Why else would you run away from a party a few seconds after you got there? If you didn't leave to call the police, then you left because you're crazy. And don't say *that* isn't true!"

Meg sat very still. Her ex–best friend was calling her crazy, and the word thundered in her ears. But Meg wasn't just listening; she was thinking about why Gracie was so terribly angry. She pictured the shabby little flat where Gracie lived. She thought of the father Gracie hadn't seen for years, and the mother who was irritable and suspicious during the few hours each day that she was at home. Linda's friendship must have meant something very special to Gracie—perhaps the beginning of a new life, much more interesting and exciting than the one she had. Now the friendship was over, and she felt cheated. She didn't care whose fault it was. She had to blame someone.

"I hate all of you!" Gracie spat out the words and turned to run.

"Wait!" Meg was on her feet and running, too.

Someone else was right behind her, but she kept her eyes on Gracie, who had darted across the lawn toward the little woods that ringed the picnic area.

Mrs. Cobbell bobbed up in front of Meg, her red hat askew. "You girls mustn't play over there!" she exclaimed. "The river is out of bounds for the picnic—polluted—no place to swim!" She shouted the last words after Meg, who had ducked around her and kept on running.

"Gracie, please wait!"

"She won't stop." Rhoda caught up to Meg and ran beside her. "She's too upset to hear you. Talk to her later, Meg."

"No!" Meg raced on. A row of forsythia bushes stretched in a golden wall ahead of her. She circled the hedge and found herself standing on the bank of the wide river. Below her, Gracie scrambled down over the steep cliff.

"What's she doing?" Rhoda puffed. "There's no place for her to go down there."

But Gracie had seen something they'd missed. A rowboat was pulled up on the shore, half in and half out of the water. As the girls watched, Gracie put one foot in the boat and pushed out with the other. The little boat floated free of the weeds.

It was an old boat, weatherbeaten, painted red.

"Oh, Gracie, don't!" Meg's head whirled. The water, the boat were exactly as she had seen them in her dream. But it was the Milwaukee River, not Lake Superior, that was carrying the little red boat away from the shore. It was Gracie, not Meg's father, who was in danger.

"I'm going for help!"

Rhoda glanced at Meg, surprised. "Why do that? She doesn't need help. Let her row for a while—maybe she'll calm down."

Meg was already running back the way she'd come.

"Mrs. Cobbell," she screamed. "Somebody! Come quick!"

But what could Mrs. Cobbell do, if Gracie was in danger of drowning? Meg rounded the row of forsythia bushes and cut diagonally through the woods. There was an entrance gate at the end of the road, with a small office beside it. Meg ran faster than she'd ever run in her life, ignoring the startled looks and shouts of her classmates as she tore past them. There had to be someone in the office who could help. There had to be!

"What's the matter, kid?" The boy in the office looked up as she burst through the door.

"A girl—in the river—needs help." Meg's teeth were chattering. "Please—hurry!"

The boy reached under the counter and picked up a telephone. He dialed swiftly and repeated the information that Meg gave him, his face grave. "You kids weren't supposed to go near the river," he said when he hung up. "Didn't your teachers tell you that? The police launch is on its way, but if your friend's okay she'll get a real bawling out when they pick her up."

What would he say if he knew Meg hadn't seen Gracie fall out of the boat but had only dreamed it? And what would Gracie say if she didn't fall out, and the police arrived to rescue her? It wasn't hard to guess the answer to that. Meg would have earned the name of tattletale forever.

But it was too late to worry. Meg thanked the boy and raced back toward the river. The picnic area was empty now, and when she passed the row of forsythia bushes she saw why. Her classmates and teachers were lined up on the edge of the bank. Far out in the middle of the river, the little red boat floated—empty. As Meg joined the crowd, one of the men teachers was wading into the river. He began to swim toward the boat.

"Oh, Meg." Rhoda's face was white under its sprinkling of freckles. "She fell in right after you left. One of the oars slipped and she reached for it and went over the side. It was awful!"

A cloud slid over the sun, and the river darkened as it had in Meg's dream. She looked down toward the bridge at the south end of the park and saw a police launch coming around the curve in the river. Her legs gave out, and she sat down hard.

There wasn't a sound from the watchers on the cliff as the launch drew close and cut its motor. One of the policemen leaned over the far side of the little red boat.

Meg closed her eyes. *Please let her be hanging on somehow,* she prayed. *Please, please, please.* She looked again as the policeman pulled Gracie's limp body from the water, then helped the teacher into the launch.

"Is she—?" Meg couldn't say the word. She pulled her knees up to her chin and put her head down.

Relieved laughter burst around her. Rhoda dragged Meg to her feet. "It's okay," Rhoda gasped. "Look, Meggie, it's okay! Gracie just sat up and hugged the man who pulled her out of the water. That's a pretty good sign, I'd say."

CHAPTER 15

"What's Your Secret?"

"Well, how was it?" Rhoda was sprawled on the front steps when Meg came home the next to the last day of school.

"I guess about fifty people told me I saved Gracie's life," Meg replied. "Isn't that wild? Even Mrs. Cobbell said it. She said no one else thought of going to the park office for help. And Mr. Nelson—he's the teacher who swam out to the boat—he said he isn't a very strong swimmer himself, and he doubted he could have helped Gracie if she was really drowning. He had to try, but he was scared. He said he could have hugged that policeman himself."

"How about Gracie? Did she tell you 'Thank you very much'?"

Meg sat down on a step and leaned back. "She didn't speak to me all day. But she looked a lot more cheerful. The kids were all making a fuss over her and teasing her about the policeman."

"I bet she loved every minute of it." Rhoda nodded wisely. "You did save her, you know. If you hadn't run when you did—" She looked at Meg. "I couldn't understand why you were so excited when she took off in that boat. I still wonder why you—"

Meg came suddenly to life. She scooped up the paper bag containing the notebooks, sneakers, and two sweaters from her cleaned-out locker. "I'd better check in," she said. "Wednesday is my mother's day off, and we usually eat early. I'll come down later, if you're going to be home."

"I'll be around," Rhoda said, looking a little puzzled. "My father's working late, so we probably won't eat for hours. If I'm not out here when you come back, knock on our door."

What a narrow escape! Meg thought as she climbed the stairs to the fourth floor. No one but Rhoda knew she had run for help *before* Gracie fell into the river. Meg had hoped her friend would have forgotten about it in the excitement of the rescue.

The apartment smelled of lemon oil and floor wax. Meg's mother was washing windows in the living room. She looked tired, but when she saw Meg she dropped her sponge into the pail beside her and stood with her hands clasped.

"Mrs. Wriston just telephoned," she said. "She wanted to thank you for saving Gracie's life yesterday. Your homeroom teacher—Mrs. What's-her-name— called and told her," she added dryly. "I don't know what's happened between you and Gracie, but I gather she isn't spreading the word herself that you did her quite a favor."

"Mrs. Cobbell." Meg felt a glow of pleasure. Her mother was looking at her the way she usually looked at Bill.

But the moment of closeness slipped away. "Well, work goes on, even with a heroine in the house," her mother said. She turned back to the windows. "Maybe we'll go out for hamburgers after I finish this," she said. "Bill should be home by then."

"Do you want some help?"

Her mother waved her off impatiently. "I just may do every window in the place while I'm at it," she said. The flat note of depression was back in her voice. "Then maybe I'll be tired enough to sleep tonight."

Meg went out to the kitchen and scooped the last of Grandma Korshak's home-baked cookies from the cookie jar.

"I'm going downstairs to talk to Rhoda," she said from the doorway. "We'll be out on the steps."

Her mother nodded without turning. "Ask her if she wants to have a hamburger with us, if you want to," she said. "I guess we can afford one more."

Rhoda accepted a couple of cookies gratefully and said she'd be glad to have supper with the Korshaks. "I'll leave my dad a note," she said. "He probably won't be home till after we get back, anyway." She pointed down the block. "Bill just came out of the store."

Bill's head was down and his shoulders were hunched in his usual slouch, but there was a jauntiness in his walk that had been missing for a few days. He must be thinking about college. The application was in the mail; commencement was next week. He was on his way.

"I'm going to miss him when he goes to Madison," Meg said.

Rhoda bit into a cookie. "I think having a big brother would be the best thing in the world," she said. "You're lucky, Meg."

They sat silently till Bill joined them on the steps. "Well, well," he said. "The fastest sprinter and the best hitter in town. Some reception committee we have here." Meg had told him all about the picnic the night before.

"Mrs. Wriston called Mama," she said shyly. "And Mama's taking us out to eat tonight. Rhoda, too."

"To celebrate your good deed?" Bill looked pleased.

"I think she's just tired. But she was glad Mrs. Wriston called. I could tell."

Rhoda leaned forward. "I still want to know about yesterday, Meggie," she said. "Remember, I asked you before? Why did you think Gracie was in danger in that boat? Why did you start running before she fell into the water?"

Meg looked away from her friend and met Bill's startled gaze.

"Before she fell in?" he repeated. "You ran for help *before* she fell in?"

"Yes, she did," Rhoda said firmly. "Meg was already out of sight, and I kept calling to her to come back. Then I turned around, and there was Gracie reaching for the oar and losing her balance. So what's your secret, Meggie?"

"Yeah, speak up," Bill said. "What's your secret?"

Meg remembered her talk with Grandma Korshak. *My secret is a window,* she thought. It sounded so uncomplicated put that way, like the title of a song. But it wasn't simple at all. Maybe if she could accept the window as Grandma did, then she could explain it to Bill and Rhoda and believe they would still love her.

"Wait here," she said. "I'll be right back."

Minutes later, when she came back downstairs, the sun had slipped behind the buildings across the street.

Brookfield Avenue had assumed its twilight calm.

"You can look at this, if you want to," Meg said. She sat down and opened the dream notebook across her knees. Slowly, she turned the pages, pointing to the dates at the top, giving Bill and Rhoda time to notice the changes in handwriting over the years, from childish scrawl to neat script. In a sometimes shaky voice, she explained what the book was and why she had written it.

"It was sort of like telling the dreams to someone. And afterward, if they came true, I could go back and see if I had everything right."

While Rhoda leaned close, Bill took the book from Meg and turned back to the first page. He read, looking up from time to time. When he had examined every page, he went back to the dream about his receiving the scholarship and read it again.

"A big tan envelope with blue lettering," he said. "I always wondered about that—even after you said you just imagined it."

"Well"—Meg was defensive—"I did, in a way."

"In a way."

"Grandma Korshak has real dreams, too," Meg told them. "She talked about them last time she was here. I guess I inherited—whatever it is—from her. But she said Mama wouldn't like to hear about dreams that come true. It would make her angry. Dad told me that, too—a long time ago. So I just kept writing in the notebook." She squirmed under her brother's unspoken question. "I couldn't tell you, either. I was afraid you'd think I was crazy. I know Gracie would have said I was crazy if I'd told her."

"You could have told me." Bill turned abruptly to Rhoda. "Well, what do *you* say, kiddo? What about our dream girl? Is she crazy?"

"Oh, no!" Rhoda looked up and down the street with shining eyes. "You know," she added, "when my dad said we were going to move again, I was so mad I cried. I liked living in New York—it was exciting. And when we got here, I thought, sure enough, it's just another old apartment building on another old street. Pure Dullsville." She shook her head in wonder. "And now, all of a sudden, there's something marvelous going on. Right here on Brookfield Avenue."

"It isn't marvelous," Meg protested. "I don't like it at all."

Rhoda paid no attention. "Meg, you *are* lucky," she said. "How could you keep quiet about such a great thing?"

Meg felt like a Frisbee, flying right up into the evening sky. She'd told her secret, had brought the notebook out of its hiding place at last, and no one was laughing. No one thought she was crazy. *Something marvelous,* Rhoda had said. *Right here on Brookfield Avenue.*

Maybe, just maybe, Rhoda was right. Meg tried to sort out her feelings. Grandma Korshak thought it was good to have a secret window. Perhaps it really was, or perhaps it was just something to get used to—like straight hair and long, narrow feet. Like having a mother who would have preferred a daughter more like herself and having a father who said writing was his life.

"Hey, we got a letter." Bill took an envelope from his shirt pocket and dropped it in Meg's lap. "It came to the store, in care of me. He's writing to Ma separately."

Meg knew without looking who "he" was. It was too soon to expect an answer to her letter, but he'd written anyway. She slipped the sheet of lined paper from the envelope.

" 'Dear kids,' " she read aloud. " 'I'm going to write to your mother tomorrow, but this is just for you. I keep wishing I hadn't left without saying good-by to you both. It was cowardly, I guess, but I was feeling bruised and sorry for myself, and I didn't feel up to any more discussions. I believe I'm doing the right thing. Will write a long letter later. Remember, I love you and I miss you. Dad.' "

In the silence that followed, Meg and Bill looked at each other and shrugged. Then Meg read the letter again, to herself. It was short, kind of stiff, and it didn't mention coming home. Nothing had changed—except she no longer hated the person who had written it. *He's lonesome, too,* she thought. *But he's all by himself, and we're together.*

Rhoda cleared her throat. "Don't hold your breath waiting for that long letter," she warned. "My mother always says she's going to write more later, but she doesn't. It takes a lot of time, I guess—doing your thing."

A window opened over their heads, and Meg looked up.

"Anybody hungry?" her mother called. "I'm coming down."

They waved and called back. Meg thrust the notebook at Rhoda. "Will you keep it in your apartment?" she asked. "I'll pick it up when we get home. Or tomorrow."

Watching Rhoda hurry up the steps, Meg realized that the notebook no longer mattered so much. "I suppose I'll tell Mama, too, someday," she said. "But not today."

Not until she was sure—absolutely sure—that being different meant being special as well. When she was certain of that, Meg thought, she'd be able to make her mother believe it, too.

About the author
Betty Ren Wright has had stories published in many magazines. She has also written 35 picture books, most of them published during the years that she was an editor for a children's book publisher. She is the author of *Getting Rid of Marjorie*, which is available as an Apple Paperback.

Ms. Wright lives with her husband in Kenosha, Wisconsin. She now devotes herself full-time to writing and free-lance editing.